For the first time in many a long year, Edward lost control of himself. He pulled her down onto his knees and wrapped both his arms close around her. As her soft breasts melted against his chest, his lips found hers and firmed in a hot embrace that sent his blood flaming like wildfire through his veins and throbbing in his throat.

As the moment's madness subsided, Samantha withdrew from his arms and stood up. She had let him kiss her out of curiosity, to see if Salverton was as cold-blooded as he pretended—and perhaps, she admitted, because she just wanted him to kiss her. She hadn't realized a simple kiss could accelerate so swiftly to passion. . . .

By Joan Smith
Published by Fawcett Books:

THE SAVAGE LORD GRIFFIN
GATHER YE ROSEBUDS
AUTUMN LOVES: An Anthology
THE GREAT CHRISTMAS BALL
NO PLACE FOR A LADY
NEVER LET ME GO
REGENCY MASQUERADE
THE KISSING BOUGH
A REGENCY CHRISTMAS: An Anthology
DAMSEL IN DISTRESS
A KISS IN THE DARK
THE VIRGIN AND THE UNICORN
KISSING COUSINS

KISSING COUSINS

Joan Smith

FAWCETT CREST • NEW YORK

A Fawcett Crest Book
Published by Ballantine Books
 Published in the United States by Ballantine Books, a division of Random House, Inc., New York, and simultaneously in Canada by Random House of Canada Limited, Toronto.

Library of Congress Catalog Card Number: 95-90429

ISBN: 0-449-22381-7

Manufactured in the United States of America

First Edition: December 1995

10 9 8 7 6 5 4 3 2 1

Chapter One

Miss Oakleigh peered from the window of a small flat on Upper Grosvenor Square to the road below. The solitude of an afternoon in late May was undisturbed by so much as a pedestrian. Sunlight cast its beam indifferently on the tall elms waving gently in the breeze, on the façades of yellow brick houses, and the cobbled street.

Her companion, Miss Donaldson, peered up from her embroidery and said, for perhaps the tenth time that afternoon, "Any sign of him yet, Samantha?"

"No," Miss Oakleigh replied in a weary voice. A frown puckered her brow as she paced to and fro in the small saloon. "And no reply to my notes. He can't be at Wanda's house."

Glancing at her niece, whom she had known for half of her own forty-four years, Miss Donaldson felt she was looking at a stranger. It was not the frown puckering Samantha's brow or the shadow in her blue eyes that caused this sensation. The blue mulled muslin gown was perfectly familiar. She had known it when it was still an ell on the shelf in Mr. Muldoon's drapery shop in Milford. The gown was a month old and had been seen many times. It looked well on Samantha's tall, elegant form.

Miss Donaldson decided it was the tousle of blond curls where one was accustomed to seeing a subdued wave pulled back from the brow that changed her niece's appearance so startlingly. It robbed the girl of her native elegance and left in its place a saucy, hoydenish air.

"What should we do, Auntie?" Samantha asked in a voice edged with fear. "It is unlike Darren to shab off without telling us. He knows we were to leave for Wiltshire today. We sent off all the servants except Mary. You don't think it has come to a runaway match with Wanda? There would be no need for that."

"I hope not," Miss Donaldson said with a tsk of dismay. "She's a decade too old for him."

"That is half her charm. And she's so very pretty, with that glossy black hair."

"Fine as a star. She bowled the lad over entirely, but Miss Burridge, next door, says the woman is nothing else but a lightskirt."

If respectability determined the weight of the skirt, Miss Donaldson's gown would weigh a ton. She was an austere-looking spinster wearing a cap with a blue ribbon, which provided the only touch of color to an otherwise gray ensemble. Her modest gown was of dove gray sarsenet, her hair and even her eyes were gray.

"I wonder if she is right," Samantha said. "Miss Burridge also said the postman stole her letter, and the butcher added the weight of his thumb to the scales. I always felt Wanda was very free in her manner, but as this was my first trip to London, I made sure it was only my provincial eye that detected a hint of scarlet."

"I told you any female who lets herself be picked up at Vauxhall is no lady."

"I was with Darren that evening. There was nothing improper in it. Wanda got separated from her friends, and that hedgebird *was* pestering her. I saw it myself."

"Hedgebirds don't pester respectable ladies. I knew what she was up to when she told us that cock-and-bull story about being afraid her cousin would force her to marry him. She was angling for an invitation to Drumquin, and failing that, she has talked that ninnyhammer of a Darren into some compromising situation in hopes he'll offer for her. How can Sir Geoffrey Bayne be trying to force her into marriage? Miss Burridge told me last night he is a married man. Her son-in-law knows him and his wife."

"I have no doubt Miss Burridge's son-in-law knows a Mr. Bayne, but who is to say it is Sir Geoffrey?"

"She said he knows Sir Geoffrey Bayne. I cannot think there are two gentlemen called Sir Geoffrey Bayne, even in London. Wanda Claridge is nothing else but his bit o' muslin. A lightskirt preying on country bumpkins! If Darren has married her, he is ruined. And no man will take a second look at *you* either, my girl."

"I don't care a fig for that. Where can he be? Darren took every penny from the sugar bowl and has been gone since eight o'clock last night." Samantha went once again to the window and glanced out. A gasp of alarm caught in her throat.

Miss Donaldson hastened to the window to see what had caused it. She saw a fat little man in a broad-brimmed white hat, a blue jacket, and kerseymere breeches pelting toward the door. The figure was more comical than frightening. "Who is he?" she asked.

"It's Mr. Townsend, the Bow Street officer. Wanda pointed him out to me on Bond Street the day she helped me buy that bonnet. He's coming *here*!"

"It may be one of the neighbors he's calling on. That Mr. Halpenny is a suspicious-looking fellow."

"But if he does come here, what shall we do?"

"Do what I've been telling you to do all along. Call on Cousin Edward and ask his advice."

There was no time for that, however. When the loud knock came at the door thirty seconds later, Samantha's cheeks blanched to white. Her knees were trembling so hard, she could hardly move to open the door.

Mr. Townsend stepped in, introduced himself, and asked the ladies their names. "I have a warrant for the arrest of Darren G. Oakleigh on a charge of theft," he announced, flourishing an official-looking piece of paper.

"What—what is he supposed to have stolen?" Samantha asked in a quavering voice.

Miss Donaldson was beyond words. She fanned herself vigorously and placed a bony hand on her heart to still its thumping.

"One thousand pounds. The charge is being pressed by Sir Geoffrey Bayne against a Miss Wanda Claridge and Mr. Oakleigh. The money was taken from the safe of the love nest Sir Geoffrey hired for Miss Claridge. The servants tell me Mr. Oakleigh forced the safe and ran off with Miss Claridge last evening. Sir Geoffrey didn't learn of it until he returned unexpectedly from the country and called on his *chère amie* this morning. Is Mr. Oakleigh at home, ma'am?"

Samantha shook her head in bewilderment. "He hasn't been home since yesterday afternoon," she said in a weak voice.

"You realize it is a criminal offense to harbor a thief, ma'am?"

"Take a look about if you wish. He's not here."

Mr. Townsend availed himself of the invitation. He strode through the little apartment, peering under beds and into clothespresses until he was satisfied that the girl was telling the truth. His practiced eye had the place pegged within a minute. It was obviously the domicile of respectable ladies in straitened circumstances. The few good pieces of furniture spoke of past grandeur, but the faded elegance had not been refurbished in a decade. Before leaving, he asked a great many questions which the ladies answered truthfully. Mr. Townsend could smell a lie a block away.

No, Mr. Oakleigh had no carriage with him except his traveling carriage, which was kept at the stable that went with the flat. Townsend had already been to the stable. The carriage and team of four had been taken out the evening before. This suggested that the culprits had left town.

Miss Donaldson had recovered her voice and explained, "We have no idea where they are, officer. We don't live here. We are only on holiday. Miss Oakleigh's aunt, Mrs. Talbot, is on vacation in the Lake District, and offered us her flat for a month—a little holiday for the youngsters. We were to leave for Wiltshire today."

"Ye've never been to London before?" he asked Miss Oakleigh. She shook her head. "That would explain it," he said. "Greenhorns," he added to himself, then said aloud, "What was the relationship between Miss Claridge and Mr. Oakleigh?"

"Friends," Samantha said grimly. "We thought she was our friend."

"The sort of friend that makes an enemy unnecessary," Townsend said with a shake of his grizzled head. "I'll not pester you further, ladies. If the lad shows up, send him to Bow Street." He adopted an avuncular tone and added, "I'll not go hard on the boy. I know who is at the bottom of this mess of potage. It's not the first time Miss Claridge, as she calls herself this month, has been in the suds."

"This month!" Samantha exclaimed. "Who was she last month?"

"That I can't tell you, but she was Nancy Hewitt a few years back, and Sally Bright before that. You don't want to have much to do with the likes of her. Good day to ye."

He bowed and took his leave.

As soon as the ladies were alone, Samantha recovered her spirits. Anger put the color back in her cheeks and fire in her eyes.

"I am going to Brighton and haul Darren back by the scruff of the neck," she declared. "And I shall give Miss Wanda Claridge—as she calls herself this month—a piece of my mind as well."

"Shocking!" Miss Donaldson said. "Why would she require so many names unless she is up to no good? I wonder what her real name is. Jane Shore, I shouldn't wonder. You think they are at Brighton? I would have thought they'd head to Drumquin."

"Wanda is forever talking up Brighton. If she had a thousand pounds in her pocket, that is where she would head. The ton is leaving London now that the Season is drawing to a close."

"They might have headed to Gretna Green," Miss Donaldson suggested with a worried glance.

"If they've gone there, it's too late to stop them. They left yesterday. I doubt it is marriage she has in her eye, Auntie. She knows we live quietly in the country, and planned to return there today. Wanda never spoke of anything but having a good time. And she had a key to Sir Geoffrey's Brighton cottage. She had been there before. She spoke highly of it."

"Surely if she robbed him, she wouldn't have the gall to go there."

"She's brazen enough for anything. And she thinks Sir Geoffrey is still in the country, I expect. Townsend mentioned he returned unexpectedly. Though with the thousand pounds, she might be at a hotel. I'll tell you one thing, she had a bathing costume made up last week, and she wouldn't be needing that at Drumquin. I shall catch the next coach to Brighton. I shan't ask you to go with me. You can stay here with Mary."

"You can't go alone on the common stage." Miss Donaldson knew when her niece's chin firmed in that mulish way she had that argument was pointless.

"I'm two and twenty. I can look after myself. Besides, I haven't enough money to hire a carriage and team and driver. I have only the bit I had in my reticule. Darren took everything else. One of us should be here to warn him of Townsend, in case he returns."

"Call on Cousin Edward," Miss Donaldson said.

"That old stick? I hardly know him. I met him

only once five years ago at Cousin Celine's wedding. He seemed astonished that I wasn't married or engaged at the ripe old age of seventeen years."

"He is your cousin—top of the trees. It won't do Darren any harm to have Cousin Edward in his camp. Lord Salverton would have great influence with the law," Miss Donaldson said with a meaningful nod of her cap. "He would move heaven and earth to keep any scandal out of the family. Very high in the instep, you must know."

Samantha drew her bottom lip between her teeth to help her make a decision. "Oh, very well. Darren will need all the help he can get, but I don't look forward to Cousin Edward's tirade when he hears what Darren has been up to."

"He'll cut up stiff. It is the price we must pay for his help. But really, you know, I think Cousin Edward will understand. He is always helpful to his relatives."

"I shall pack a bandbox to take with me. I plan to go to Brighton, whether Cousin Edward approves or not. I expect I shall be back tomorrow, Auntie, and then we can leave this horrid city. I wish we had never come to London. I look forward to the peace and quiet of Drumquin. I never thought I would say that!"

"I only hope we won't have to share Drumquin with Miss Claridge."

"Or Mrs. Darren Oakleigh. If Wanda has got him to a vicar, we are finished."

On this dismal speech she went into the bedroom and packed up a few necessities, and Miss Donaldson spent a moment thinking of Lord Salverton. It would be a wonderful thing indeed if Cousin Edward should develop a tendre for Samantha. It seemed unlikely enough on the face of it, but if rumor was to be believed, there had been a time when Lord Salverton was not so nice as he now appeared.

Samantha placed on her head a high poke bonnet with coquelicot ribbons that Wanda had assured her was the latest jet. It certainly caused heads to turn, in any case. This concoction was toned down by a plain merino cape over her gown. Once dressed, she took her leave of Miss Donaldson and went into the street to search for a hackney cab.

She was soon alighting in front of a veritable mansion on Berkeley Square. The yellow brick house was enormous. It towered proudly over its neighbors. Its severe geometry and obvious prosperity seemed in keeping with its owner. Everything that wasn't brick gleamed in the fading sunlight. The windows sparkled, the brass door knocker sparkled, even the globe of the lamp outside the door sparkled. The heavy, cold lion's-head knocker emitted a sonorous sound when she used it.

The toplofty butler who answered her knock was enough to make a prince tremble. He looked as if he had been weaned on a lemon.

He took one look at the garish ribbons on her bonnet and said, "Can I help you, miss?"

Samantha pokered up at that demeaning "miss." "I want to see Lord Salverton, if you please," she replied.

The butler looked down his long, parsnip nose and said, "His lordship is occupied. Would you care to leave a message, or perhaps speak to his secretary?"

Samantha drew a deep breath, lifted her chin,

and said, "No, I would not care to leave a message or speak to his secretary. It is excessively important that I speak to my cousin at once. Tell him Miss Oakleigh, from Drumquin, requires a moment of his time."

Luten's ire subsided at the word "cousin." His lordship had droves of them. No cousin was ever turned from the door without first having a hearing.

"Please step in, Miss Oakleigh," the butler said in a somewhat less frigid voice than before, and held the door. "I shall see if his lordship is free for a moment."

Samantha peered around an entrance hallway that belonged in a castle. A lake of black and white marble stretched before her. Its surroundings were reflected in its shining surface, like a real lake. In the near distance, a gracefully curved stairway led up to a balcony. Disapproving marble statues glowered down at her from their niches in the wall. On an ornate gilt table, a bouquet of flowers roughly a yard in diameter bowed in the slight breeze from the doorway. Their aroma blended with that of beeswax and turpentine.

The butler disappeared into the depths of the long hallway and reappeared again a moment later.

"Right this way, Miss Oakleigh," he said, beckoning her forward.

Samantha followed the butler down the hall. Her shoes made a light clicking sound on the marble floor. She walked carefully to avoid slipping on the highly polished surface.

The butler opened a paneled door and said, "Miss Oakleigh, your lordship," and Samantha stepped into the study to face her toplofty cousin.

Chapter Two

A well-barbered black head, sleek as a wet seal, lifted from the paper Lord Salverton had been perusing, and Samantha found herself being examined by a pair of steel gray eyes. The face was as she remembered it from five years before. Handsome, with a well-shaped nose and firm jaw, but the features were marred by an expression not far removed from disdain.

Lord Salverton, always the perfect gentleman, rose and bowed. "Nice to see you again, Cousin. I can spare you a moment," he said in polite if not warm accents. "Miss Oakleigh, is it not?"

Samantha forgot to curtsy, which was a grave omission in Salverton's view. She was distracted by the elegance of her cousin's toilette. At five o'clock he was already dressed for the evening. How Darren would love a burgundy jacket like that! It clung to Salverton's broad shoulders. At his throat, a discreet ruby gleamed from a fall of lace. The gem picked up the hues of the jacket.

"Yes, it's Samantha," she said, compounding the felony by thrusting her first name on him. "I have come for your help." Salverton's nostrils pinched in disapproval. "That is—your advice," she added uncertainly.

"Pray be seated, Cousin," he asked, wafting a shapely hand in the direction of an oak chair in front of the desk. He waited until she was seated before sitting down himself in an armchair whose carved excesses suggested a throne. The desk was as wide as a dinner table, but not so cluttered. It held only a chased silver ink pot, pens, a leather address book, and a blotting paper on which rested a report bearing a government seal. The oak-lined room was handsomely furnished and tidy almost to excess.

While Samantha glanced nervously around, Salverton's experienced eye studied the coquelicot ribbons on her bonnet and mentally disparaged them. But then, it was no new thing for a country cousin to go overboard on her first foray into the shops of London. A pity, for the face was quite tolerable. The eyes especially. That particular shade of blue, deeper than forget-me-nots, lighter than sapphires, always appealed to him. And those long lashes were extraordinary.

Samantha leaned forward and said in a conspiratorial voice, "The thing is, Cousin, my brother Darren—you remember Darren?"

"The heir to Drumquin. I remember him very well. He struck me as a sensible lad, though I haven't seen him for a few years."

"Five years. Cousin Celine's wedding, at Bath."

"Just so. Celine married a solicitor. I think she might have done better, with a dot of seven thousand. And Darren is in London with you?"

"Well, yes. That is, we came to London together for a holiday."

"You should have come sooner. The Season is just

ending. There were some very interesting partis this year, too."

"Actually we came a month ago."

Salverton pokered up at this. He would not have objected to steering his young cousin toward an advantageous match. He took a keen interest in the welfare of all his large and extended family.

"Then you are not seeking my advice regarding a place to stay, or an introduction to the ton."

"No. We had planned to leave today actually."

"Ah, you have come to say good-bye," he said. This was marginally better than not saying good-bye. At least they were paying some token homage to the head of the extended family. "It would have been more useful had you come to me when you arrived. Another time . . ."

"I doubt there will be another time. It is this time that I need your advice, Cousin," Samantha said, and opened her budget to Lord Salverton. It did not occur to her to attempt any tampering with the truth. She told her tale frankly, in words with no bark on them.

He listened as one in a trance as she spoke of lightskirts and gudgeons and Johnnie Raws and take-ins. It sounded like bad fiction to this upright lord, that a pair of adults could behave so foolishly as the Oakleighs had. Yet he could not condemn them entirely. Her story called up painful memories of another misspent youth. She spoke of visits to Vauxhall and Astley's Circus, of shopping and tours of Exeter Exchange, all, apparently, in the company of some female called Wanda Claridge. That Salverton was unfamiliar with the name told him the woman was unknown to society.

When she was finished with her story, he said

only, "Why didn't you make your bows like a *lady* instead of capering about town like a hoyden?"

"Good gracious, Edward, I am not on the catch for a parti. I am hardly a deb! I am well past that!"

Lord Salverton found room in his mind for displeasure at her usurping his christian name without permission. "My friends call me Salverton," he said through thin lips. "My relations more usually call me Cousin Edward. Am I to understand you have already chosen a parti, Cousin? Would I know the gentleman?"

"I am not engaged, though I have not entirely given up the notion of marrying when Darren brings home a bride. And that is why I came to you. I fear Darren has been caught by Wanda. Aunt Donaldson thinks she has shanghaied him off to Gretna Green, but *I* think they have gone to Brighton."

"To be married?" he asked in alarm. Darren Oakleigh had inherited Drumquin upon his papa's death. A handsome estate of seventy-five hundred acres, and a good income. Salverton had mentally assigned him to his cousin, Aurora Semple, who would make her bows in two years time.

"Well, I am not so sure it is marriage they have in mind."

Salverton was somewhat reassured by this. "If it is only an—er—affair," he said, "I trust he will be discreet."

"He won't have much to say about it. Wanda leads him around by the halter, and she doesn't know the meaning of the word discreet. The thing is, Cousin, they took some money that didn't belong to them, though I don't believe for one moment that Darren knew that. I wager Wanda told him Sir

Geoffrey owed her the thousand pounds. She was Sir Geoffrey's *chère amie* as it turns out, only, of course, none of us had any notion of it."

Salverton listened, dumbfounded.

"The story she told us," Samantha continued, "was that he was her cousin, and trying to force her into marriage. But Miss Burridge, who lives in the flat above Aunt Talbot, who lent us her place on Upper Grosvenor Square, you know, says Sir Geoffrey is already married. Miss Burridge is a regular Jeremiah. She would paint the Archbishop of Canterbury black if she could, but as it turns out, it is no more than the truth about Sir Geoffrey. He says the money was stolen, in any case. He reported it to Bow Street. We had a call from a Mr. Townsend, which is why I came to you for advice."

Lord Salverton's face turned from tan to rosy red, then faded to something very like the color of a slug as this tale unfolded. An Oakleigh, kin to the Marquess of Salverton, being sought for theft! Capering about the countryside with a known harlot, and possibly in danger of marrying her, bringing her into the family!

This would have been enough to induce an apoplexy in his lordship at the best of times. This present May was the worst of times for such news. Not only was he on the verge of offering his hand and title (though perhaps not his heart) to Lady Louise St. John, eldest and best-dowered daughter of the Duke of Derwent; of equal importance, after long years of service he was being considered for elevation to the Tory Cabinet. The worst possible time for a scandal!

"Why the devil didn't you come to me sooner!" he said in a voice several tones higher than usually heard under Salverton's noble roof. He didn't notice the strength of his voice, but the word "devil" struck his ear amiss. It was not one he approved of in others, and certainly not in himself, especially in front of a lady. Even a lady wearing coquelicot ribbons.

"We came to London to have a good time. Some fun, you know. There seemed no point in contacting you."

The worst of this facer was that she didn't even mean it as an insult. Salverton swallowed his ire and said in his most laconic accents, "Our views on what constitutes a good time do appear to be at odds. I could not have introduced you to lightskirts, to be sure. But there is no point crying over spilled milk. What have you done about Darren's situation? Of course you've hired a lawyer."

"I never thought of that," she said, blinking her big blue eyes in surprise. "We never had anything to do with the law before, you see, except to bail out our coachman when he was drunk as a Dane and drove into the Shaws' back porch, which is why we came to you. Whom would you recommend, Cousin?" she asked in a frightened voice that he felt suitable to the occasion.

"I'll send a note off to my man, Withers."

As soon as the words were out of his mouth, he began to have second thoughts. To be taking the case to court was as good as announcing it in the journals. There might still be some way to wrap up the dirty linen. Sir Geoffrey might be induced to drop the case if the thousand pounds were returned, and perhaps some small political perquisite thrown in to ensure his silence.

"Would you mind speaking to him for me?" she

asked. "I feel my best chance of finding Darren is Brighton. I am eager to be off."

"Why Brighton?" he asked in trepidation. The half of polite London would be flocking to Brighton as soon as the Season closed.

"Because Wanda had a bathing costume made up."

Salverton waited for the significance of this. "Yes?"

"She would have no need of that in London, so I am sure she went to Brighton, and I have a fair idea where she is staying. Sir Geoffrey used to take her to a cottage he owns there, just outside of town. To visit his mama, she *said*. She had a key to the cottage."

"Trespassing on top of all the rest!"

"Or they might be at a hotel. Miss Donaldson thinks so, but I am not so sure Wanda would waste the blunt. She is pretty tight-fisted when it is her own money. Or, in this case, Sir Geoffrey's. I paid for everything when I was out with her a few times without Darren. It was only two ices and the fare for a hackney cab, but she never opened her purse. You would think it was welded shut," she said with an air of grievance.

Salverton listened with a frown pleating his brow. "By all means, go to Brighton. Find Darren and drag him back to town. Meanwhile, I shall have a word with Withers."

"The problem is," she said, "we gave Darren all our money. If you could lend me a few guineas to take the coach, naturally I shall repay you."

"The coach! You can't travel on the coach. Take your carriage."

"Darren took it as well," she said, and shrugged her shoulders.

"Good God! Is there no end to his folly, leaving you and Miss Donaldson stranded, penniless, away from home. I'll lend you some money. Be sure you take a couple of footmen with you."

Samantha uttered a weary sigh. "We dispatched them this morning. We were to go home today, you see."

"I'll send a few of my men with you and Miss Donaldson."

"Auntie won't be coming. Someone must stay here in case Darren shows up."

Salverton sat, shaking his head in disbelief. It was becoming increasingly clear that the whole bunch of them were not only green as grass, but mad as well. The chit couldn't go alone, and he had no wish to drag any of his other female relatives into the business. He trembled to think what new folly his cousin would stumble into if he let the girl go scrambling off to Brighton alone in a public conveyance in that garish bonnet. There was nothing else to do. He would have to go with her and make sure the matter was contained within the family.

It would mean missing Louise's dinner party, but he had cautioned her he would have to leave early, so he could say an emergency meeting had been called. Salverton considered himself an honest man, but even his strict code found room for a social lie. It would spare Louise worry. He would be home to take her to the opera tomorrow night, and for her ball the next evening. He couldn't miss that ball. If all went well, the Duke of Derwent would announce the betrothal of his eldest daughter to the Marquess of Salverton.

"I'll go with you," Salverton said in a voice more resigned than eager.

Samantha leapt to her feet as if he had struck her. "Oh, no! I would not dream of putting you to so much bother, Cousin. Just lend me a few guineas."

"No female cousin of mine is going alone on the coach to a strange city. You can't stay alone overnight in a hotel."

"But I can hardly stay with you in a hotel," she pointed out reasonably.

"You are my young cousin. I am your ad hoc guardian for this occasion," he said, but a pink flush crept up from his collar. What would Louise say if she ever heard of this? "In any case, we shan't be staying overnight. We'll take my carriage, find Darren, haul him back, and arrange matters with Bayne. We'll be back by morning. I have a few notes to write before leaving. I was just working on this budget report for the prime minister. It is due this week."

"The prime minister! Really!" she exclaimed, showing the proper degree of awe.

"Lord Liverpool counts on me to a considerable extent," he said as modestly as the words allowed. When she just smiled, he added, "You might as well remove your pelisse. This will take a few moments."

While Samantha did not relish spending so many hours in Salverton's company, she knew his carriage would be preferable to the coach. And it would be well to have a gentleman with her, too, for finding Darren and Wanda might require a deal of legwork. She took off her cape and spread it over the back of her chair.

"It is very kind of you, Cousin," she said. "I meant only to ask your advice, and perhaps borrow a little money. Miss Donaldson said you would know what to do, and I see she was right."

Salverton smiled at this sensible speech. It was at this point that he noticed his cousin was remarkably well preserved for a lady in her twenties. In fact, she was prettier than she had been five years before, at Celine's wedding. A late bloomer. Her figure, especially, had blossomed remarkably. He couldn't remember her having such full, lush breasts before. The face was also pretty, but he would ask her to change her bonnet before leaving.

He rang for his butler and called for his traveling carriage. This done, he drew out a sheet of crested vellum and began to write. Samantha sat and watched him as his pen made bold strokes across the page.

"Who is Louise?" she asked.

His head rose and his steely eyes stared at her. "Is it the custom in Milford for a lady to read a gentleman's private correspondence?" he asked sarcastically.

"I was not reading the letter, Cousin! Only the name. Good gracious, don't tell me she is a lightskirt!" she exclaimed.

His gray eyes turned a shade darker. "Certainly not! She is the eldest daughter of the Duke of Derwent, if you must know."

"Is she your sweetheart?" the incorrigible lady asked.

"I hope to marry her."

"Is she pretty?"

"She is considered tolerably handsome."

"Oh, a marriage of convenience," Samantha said. "Of course. I should have guessed."

Salverton's jaw quivered in indignation.

She immediately lost interest in the letter and amused herself by opening her reticule and stacking up her shillings and pence on the edge of his desk to facilitate counting them.

As Salverton applied a wafer to seal his letter, the butler came to tell him his carriage was waiting.

Salverton and Samantha went out to a handsome black, crested carriage drawn by a team of four high-stepping bays.

"We shall be there in no time," Samantha said, admiring the team.

Salverton held the door while she scampered in. "First we shall stop and have a word with Miss Donaldson, while you change your bonnet," he said.

"Miss Donaldson knows I shall be going to Brighton," Samantha replied, fingering the velvet squabs of the carriage and running her eye over the glitter of what was probably silver appointments. "I brought my bandbox with me."

"You will want to change your bonnet, in any case."

"The servants have gone on ahead to Drumquin with most of our trunks," she said, although she had, in fact, kept another bonnet behind, as this one was considered too fine to subject to the long journey home. "You don't seem to realize, Cousin, speed is of the essence if we hope to keep Darren out of Newgate."

Jail! He could almost hear the door clang, and the death knell of his own aspirations. Salverton was perfectly alive to the urgency of the matter and decided no one who mattered would see the garish bonnet.

"Spring 'em, Foley," he called to his coachman, and the carriage lurched into motion.

Chapter Three

The first glimmering that this trip was not to go as smoothly as Salverton hoped occurred before they got out of London. In fact, it was at the corner of Piccadilly that Lord Carnford, a fellow Tory and colleague, recognized Salverton's carriage and signaled his coachman to stop.

Salverton uttered a mild profanity, apologized, and said to Samantha, "Sit in the shadows and don't speak."

Samantha crouched in the farthest corner as Carnford hopped out of his carriage and advanced to the window of Salverton's rig. Before nightfall, even the darkest corner was not very dark, however, so she turned her head aside, hoping to conceal her face by her bonnet.

"Glad I bumped into you, Salverton," Carnford said. "I wonder if you would mind delivering my apologies to his grace. I was to dine at Derwent House this evening, but I have had a frantic note from my aunt Hettie. It seems her husband has suffered a stroke—died this afternoon. She needs me to handle the arrangements for her. Derwent will understand. I wrote my apologies, of course, but did not take time to give a reason."

"I'm very sorry to hear of your trouble, Carnford,

but it happens I had to cancel the dinner party myself."

"Indeed?" Carnford waited, fully expecting to hear a tragedy outpacing his own, for he knew Salverton would not willingly offend the duke.

"A family emergency," Salverton said briefly.

Carnford's sharp eyes strayed over his friend's shoulder to the fetching blond lady trying to hide in the corner. His jaw fell an inch. "Ah, just so," he said in a high, disbelieving voice. Salverton with a lightskirt! He wouldn't have believed it if he hadn't seen her with his own eyes. Lord Salty was back to his old tricks! A reckless grin formed on his lips and he said in a low, insinuating voice, "Mum's the word, old chap."

Salverton replied coolly, "This is my cousin, Miss Oakleigh, from Drumquin." Samantha pulled herself farther into the corner, trying to disappear. "Don't you want to meet Lord Carnford, Cousin," Salverton said grimly.

"I am certainly eager to meet your *cousin*." Carnford leered.

Samantha leaned forward and smiled. The setting sun shone on her garish bonnet, and illuminated her pretty face, with a few wayward curls slipping over her cheeks. "Ever so pleased to meet you, milord," she said with an uncomfortable smile.

"The pleasure is mutual, Miss Oakleigh," Carnford said, and went, laughing, to his carriage.

Salverton turned on his cousin in wrath. "Ever so pleased to meet you!" he exploded. "Where the devil did you pick up that ill-bred phrase? You sounded like a lightskirt." In his overwrought condition he failed to notice he had used improper language again.

"I daresay I had it of Wanda," she said in a small voice. "All her friends say it. I thought it was the smart, London way of greeting, and didn't want your friend to think me a flat. I'm sorry if I embarrassed you, Cousin."

"Embarrassment doesn't begin to cover it. In future, pray use proper English if we meet anyone else."

"Would you like me to sit on the floor?" she asked. "I could pull this blanket over my—"

"Certainly not! Damn Carnford and his long nose!"

He jerked the drawstring and the carriage proceeded on its way. Salverton comforted himself that at least Carnford wasn't going to the duke's house that evening. By tomorrow he would be back himself to explain the matter to Louise.

"Did he think I was a lightskirt?" Samantha asked.

"Yes. No! No, of course not. You shouldn't say—you shouldn't even know about such things."

"I am two and twenty, Cousin. And I think he *did* take me for your bit of muslin. As your match with Lady Louise is a marriage of convenience, surely it is not unusual that you should have a woman on the side."

"It is not a marriage of convenience!"

"You called her tolerably handsome. A man in love doesn't say that—unless she is actually an antidote. Is that the case?"

"You have a strange notion of my taste! I am hardly in a position where I must marry an antidote to lend me cachet."

"No, you need not, but I wager a duke's eldest daughter is well dowered."

"It is not cream-pot love. I have money and estates of my own."

"You are also possessed of an overweening ambition. I know the duke is very important, for one hears his name even in Milford."

"I happen to be very fond of Lady Louise," Salverton said coldly.

"Well, I am sorry. If Lady Louise shares your feelings, no doubt she will have a good laugh at this little contretemps."

Salverton's hopes did not soar so high as to hope for even a smile. Louise might, if she were caught in a good mood, forgive and commiserate. She would feel, as he did himself, that it was unfortunate. Though, as he considered it, it had been funny to see Carnford's jaw drop. A reluctant smile tugged at his lips. Besides, no one would believe it if Carnford were so indiscreet as to broadcast the tale. The Marquess of Salverton was not the devil-may-care sort of fellow to keep a lightskirt when he was courting a lady. But if anyone did believe it, at least they would have heard his *chère amie* was uncommonly pretty.

His carriage was recognized by two other acquaintances as he drove out of London. Brighton would be full of the ton as well. It was beginning to seem a good idea to stable his rig upon arrival there and hire an unmarked carriage.

Once on the highway to Brighton, they did not meet anyone else Salverton recognized, but at their rate of speed, they did pass a few carriages, and no doubt his crest was noticed.

Samantha paid little heed to the traffic. She gazed out the window at the swaying trees and setting sun that turned the sky a pretty peach color and gilded the rooftops, until the countryside looked like something from a book of fairy tales.

"It's really quite lovely, isn't it?" she said.

Salverton glanced out the window and said, "As soon as we reach Brighton, I'll stable this rig and hire a plain carriage."

"I've been a dreadful nuisance to you," Samantha said. "Why do you not just go home and let me find Darren and Wanda?"

"It would not be fitting to abandon a lady in distress."

For the next hour he asked Samantha questions about the welfare of their various relations. He was struck at the difference in their views of what constituted success. So long as relatives had married and were not living in penury, Samantha seemed to think they were doing well. She spoke with pride of someone he could not quite recall having set up a carriage, and of Cousin Francis Talbot having bought a small property near Bath.

"Why Bath?" he demanded. "Cousin Francis is a solicitor. He would do better in London. I could send some government business his way."

"His wife's mama is ailing. She makes her home with them, and they wanted her to be near Bath for the waters."

"He'll not make a name for himself in Bath. It seems a hard sacrifice to make for the sake of his wife's mama," he said, dissatisfied.

"But Francis loves Miriam, you see. He wants her to be happy, and she wants to have her mama where she can help her. Besides, he does very well in the way of wills and settling estates with all the older people there," she explained.

"Francis had great potential. Honors in two subjects at Oxford, as I recall. He should have gone into politics. He might have been a cabinet minister."

"I doubt he would be as happy as he is. Being a cabinet minister isn't that important to some people, Cousin."

This was like telling a Rothschild that money wasn't important. Salverton couldn't understand how any man would not choose to be at the helm of the ship of state. What greater accomplishment had life to offer? His own ambition was to be prime minister one day. He was about to explain this to his cousin, when she stifled a yawn and snuggled into the corner to sleep.

"The sun has nearly set," she said. "It's been such a nerve-racking day that I feel sleepy."

Salverton realized that he was likely to be up most of the night, and closed his eyes. He pondered their discussion as he tried to doze off. How could people be so unambitious? Overweening ambition, Miss Oakleigh had said. Was it immoderately ambitious of him to want to use his God-given talents to help make England a better place, and to give himself a place in the history books while he was about it?

He thought, too, of Lady Louise and what she would do if rumors of this trip reached her ears. She would be demmed unhappy. He must make sure Louise didn't get a look at Samantha, or she'd never believe it was all innocent. Carnford had taken one look and jumped to the obvious conclusion. A lady as pretty as Samantha had to be extra careful. If he'd let her come here alone, she would have had men falling over themselves in their eagerness to "help" her.

And she was such a greenhead, she would have taken them at their word. She was completely out of her depth in the city. A feeling of protectiveness welled up in him as he watched her in the fading twilight, her horrid bonnet askew and her long eyelashes fanning her cheeks. She looked about ten years old. He unfolded the blanket and tenderly arranged it over her lap. The carriage had grown chilly as the sun set.

They reached Brighton at eleven o'clock that night. Salverton directed his coachman to drive to a stable. Samantha woke up, covered her lips in a yawn, and said, "Are we here?" She noticed Salverton had placed the blanket over her and was surprised, but she didn't mention it.

"We're changing carriages," he said.

"You mean horses?"

"That, too."

When the change was made, he said to Samantha, "You know the whereabouts of this house Sir Geoffrey owns?"

"It is just to the east of Brighton, where the Marine Parade changes into—whatever it changes into. I cannot recall the name of the road. It is less than halfway to Rottingdean. Is that not a horrid name for a village? One imagines a dead dean decomposing." Seeing that Salverton was not interested in her imagination, she added, "The cottage is right on the sea."

"Does it have a name?"

"Yes," she said, and drew her brows together in a hard frown.

"Well, what is it?" he asked impatiently.

"I am trying to think, if you'll just be quiet," she said with matching impatience.

Salverton glared, but she was paying him no heed. She had screwed her eyes shut to aid concentration.

"It has something to do with old Roman statues, like those damaged ones in your house," she said.

"My statues are Greek!"

"You need not apologize, Cousin. No one would know the difference if you'd only get them patched up."

It seemed pointless to inform her that the Greek originals, even when damaged by time, were preferable to Roman copies. "Surely Sir Geoffrey hasn't the poor taste to call his cottage the Parthenon, or the Temple of Diana, or some such thing?"

"No, it wasn't that. I have it! The Laurels." Salverton blinked, wondering at such a modest name, when she had been speaking of classical antiquities. "Like the crowns of leaves they used to wear in those ancient times. Or was that bay leaves? In any case, the cottage is called The Laurels, so it should be easy to find. But before we leave, I fear I must ask you to stop somewhere for a moment."

"It has been a longish trip. A cup of coffee or a glass of wine would not go amiss. Perhaps a bite, as we missed dinner."

"That would be nice, but what I mean is I have to relieve myself," she replied bluntly.

Salverton stared. "I shall ask John Groom to stop at an inn for refreshment," he said in a damping voice. Really! These country girls!

"I'm sure it is nothing to be ashamed of, Cousin," she said. "Don't you have to go, too? If God hadn't wanted us to—"

He raised a hand to interrupt her latest solecism.

"I take your meaning. It is not necessary to draw me a picture." Hoyden! his glare said.

Her answering glare said, Prig!

In this unpromising mood they went to an inn to refresh and relieve themselves. Salverton chose a modest establishment where he was unlikely to meet anyone he knew. He hustled his guest into a private parlor and ordered dinner while she attended to necessities.

Samantha returned to find the table set with a raised partridge pie, cold ham, a roasted fowl, potatoes, and a plentiful array of vegetables. Her appetite had been in abeyance, but when she saw the food she realized she was hungry and they both enjoyed an excellent dinner. They finished a bottle of wine between them.

At the meal's end, Salverton was in a much better mood. They would be at The Laurels within the half hour. He'd ring a peal over Darren, hustle him back to London—probably have to give Wanda some money to keep her quiet—and call on Lady Louise early in the morning to make his peace with her. He'd have the morning to finish his report for Liverpool.

The evening had been unusual, but not without some pleasure. A rescue mission of this sort seldom fell in Salverton's way. He usually helped his relatives by procuring them positions or arranging a desirable match, without much personal inconvenience. He was aware of a pleasant sense of excitement, almost of daring as he offered Samantha his arm to lead her out to the carriage. He was even beginning to think the coquelicot ribbons were not so very gaudy.

He had a change of heart when he saw Mr. Herbert, another political colleague, entering a private parlor with a young lady not his wife. Mr. Herbert! He was fifty years old if he was a day, and the chit not a day over twenty. What was the world coming to? Fortunately Herbert didn't spot him, but it made Salverton aware of the apparent impropriety of this mission, and urged him to keep his guard up.

He was happy to reach the safety of his carriage without seeing anyone else he knew.

Chapter Four

As Salverton looked at his groom standing by the hired carriage, it occurred to him that the ton would recognize Foley on sight. To see him on the perch of this somewhat dilapidated rig would cause curiosity as to the occupant. Those with the true evangelical spirit for gossip would peer inside, see himself and his cousin, and assume the worst. He must be rid of his coachman and hire a driver from Winkler's stable.

Salverton explained the matter in quite different terms when he spoke to his groom.

"The carriage was making a rattling sound all the way from London," he invented. "I'd like you to go over it and see what is amiss. Just take me to Winkler's. I'll hire a driver there for a brief stop I have to make just beyond Brighton. When you've looked over my own rig, we'll meet you back here."

"You're returning to London tonight, then?" Foley asked.

"Yes." He glanced at Samantha, who was beginning to show fatigue after her busy day. He realized that he was tired himself. By the time they found Darren and Wanda and settled matters, it would be one or two o'clock. With Darren to chaperon his sister, there would be no impropriety in remaining overnight. "No," he said. "We'll put up at a hotel, as it is so late, and return tomorrow morning."

"Just as you say, your lordship. Where will you be staying, and what time do you want your rig at the door?"

"The Curzon at eight."

They were driven back to the stable to find no drivers were to be had at that hour of the night. Salverton was a good customer, however, and Winkler wished to oblige him.

"I know a lad who turns his hand to a spot of driving from time to time. An excellent whip. Jonathon Sykes is your man. I'll send for him. He'll be here in no time."

Salverton agreed. "No time" stretched to half an hour, but eventually Sykes appeared, arrayed not in a coachman's outfit but in a black evening jacket with wadded shoulders and a nipped-in waist. He was a well-set-up, handsome rogue with blond curls and a laughing blue eye. He bowed punctiliously while his eyes slewed to examine Samantha.

"Your lordship. Jonathon Sykes, at your service," he said.

This rogue in an evening suit sitting on his box would cause more curiosity than his own groom. Salverton turned a wrathful eye to Joe Winkler.

"I can lend Sykes a coachman's coat and hat," he said apologetically. "This is to be a driving job, Jonathon," he explained to his friend, then went on to speak to Salverton. "Jonathon is a jack-of-all-trades."

Sykes wrenched his gaze from Samantha to expound on his versatility. "I went into service at the age of seven, when my ma and pa died, bless their souls. Started out as backhouse boy at Lord

Egremont's and worked up from underfootman to butler, and even did a spot of clerking when the occasion demanded. I can read and write as well as a bishop. His lordship especially commended me on my penmanship. But I always had a love of the stables. I can drive anything, anywhere, anytime."

"May one inquire why you left Lord Egremont, when you were making such strides in your career?" Salverton asked.

"He upped and died, didn't he?"

"Sykes knows the neighborhood like the back of his hand," Winkler mentioned.

"Do you know a place called The Laurels, between here and Rottingdean?" Salverton asked.

"The wee thatched cottage belonging to Sir Geoffrey Bayne? I know it h'intimately. Many's the time I've taken a party to The Laurels for a bit of a frolic. A great one for parties, Sir Geoffrey. I could have you there in twenty minutes, your lordship."

It was this that induced Salverton to hire Sykes against his better judgment. He wanted to get to The Laurels as quickly as possible. "Change your outfit, then, and let us get on with it."

Sykes cleared his throat. "There's a matter of remuneration, your lordship. Not to appear mercenary, but we wasn't all born with a silver spoon in our craw."

"A guinea," Salverton said, choosing what he considered a generous sum.

Sykes quirked one eyebrow in derision. "I was torn away from a game that was likely to make me a richer man than that."

"Very well, two guineas."

"Taking into account there's not another driver to be had and your lordship must be in an almighty rush to get to The Laurels, and considering the law of supply and demand—I was thinking five guineas.

"Three. Take it or be damned."

"Three it is, sir. You do realize Sir Geoffrey ain't at The Laurels? I heard he's let it to a young lad—for his parents, they are saying about town."

Salverton assumed the young lad was Darren, and his parents a pretext. If gossip flew on such silver wings as this in Brighton, it was indeed urgent to remove Darren at once. "That's quite all right. I know Sir Geoffrey is in London."

"Just trying to save you h'exasperation, your lordship. I know all about h'exasperation."

"I'm rapidly learning about it," Salverton said dampingly, and went to have a word with Foley.

Sykes, undeterred, continued chatting with Samantha as he removed his jacket, folded it up neatly, set his hat on top of it, and handed them both to Winkler. Before long he had the gist of her story, and was contemplating how to milk it to his best advantage. He put on the hat and coat the proprietor handed him and hopped up on the box, setting his own vestments carefully beside him. Even a misshapen hat and bulky coat didn't completely conceal his physical charms.

"A trot, a canter, or a gallop, your lordship?" he inquired from the perch when Salverton returned. Sykes had no intention of hopping about and holding doors for his high-and-mighty lordship.

"You're the expert. Just get us there and back as quickly as possible without risking an accident."

A burst of Jovian laughter rumbled from Jonathon Sykes's throat. "H'accident! You've no fear of that with Jonathon Sykes holding the reins. 'Twas

Lord Alvanley himself who dubbed me the finest fiddler he ever did see—and Lord Alvanley would know about fiddling."

When Salverton held the carriage door for his cousin, he noticed she was wearing an insouciant smile. "An original," she said.

"Trying extraordinarily hard to be one. His tongue certainly runs at a trot. We shall test his fiddling before granting him the palm."

Even Salverton had to admit the carriage set off without so much as a small lurch. The trip out of Brighton was accomplished with expedition. Salverton's attention was distracted by Samantha's chatter.

"I wonder if Darren is the young man who is at The Laurels," she said. "If he and Wanda are there, I would have thought they'd keep away from Brighton. He doesn't know the money was stolen, but she knows it."

"It has been obvious for some time the woman has no sense. I expect she's been into town spending her ill-got gains."

"We should have asked Sykes. I wager he would know Wanda by sight, as she summers here."

"The less information we impart to Sykes, the better. He not only knows everything; he tells everything. I should have told Winkler not to reveal my identity."

"He does chatter," she agreed, "but it's a good feeling knowing Sykes is so clever." She turned her gaze out the window, wondering if she should confess to having told Sykes more than discretion warranted.

Salverton felt a little spurt of anger at her thoughtless comment. It was not Sykes but himself who was going to such pains to help her. She had not called *him* clever.

After another mile she said, "I thought we would see the sea from the road. The Laurels is on the sea."

Salverton glanced out at a vista of meadows backed by a stand of waving trees on one side, and an open field on the other. "The road curves. The sea will come in sight presently," he said.

"Oh, I'm sure Sykes knows what he is about."

"Have you ever seen the sea, Cousin?"

"Until the glimpse of it I had tonight at Brighton, I have seen only the Bristol Channel. The glimpse was lovely. The white moon shining on the black water—so romantic. Papa took me to Bristol once when he was there on business. We were at the docks in the morning. It was not at all romantic. Being in the middle of England, we're far from the ocean at Milford, but you must not think us provincial. We go frequently to Bath."

They continued peering out the windows for a view of the sea. After a mile, Salverton realized this was not the sea road and pulled the drawstring.

"It seems Sykes oversold himself," he said, not without a trace of satisfaction. "He may know Brighton like the back of his hand, but he obviously doesn't know the environs."

The carriage glided to a smooth stop and within seconds Sykes appeared at the window. He didn't wait for a question, but spoke at once.

"I know what you're going to say," he said, smiling.

"You do mind reading as well?" Salverton inquired.

"No, your lordship. After h'investigation, I concluded there's nothing in it. It's a bogus sham. But I fancy I know what's troubling you. You're wondering why you don't see water. I've taken a shortcut."

"I fail to see how there can be a shortcut when the road from Brighton to Rottingdean is straight. The shortest distance between two points—"

Jonathon nodded to indicate his knowledge of geometry, and spoke on before Salverton had finished his lecture.

"You've not heard of the construction work going on. I wager it's not important enough to be bruited about London, but nothing else is spoken of in Brighton. There is a detour set up that takes you four miles out of your way. I've avoided it by taking this back road a mile north of the main road. I'll have us back on the main road before you can say Jack Robinson, and the little lady will have a fine view of the moon shining on the water."

"How did you know!" Samantha exclaimed in delight. "I believe you *are* a mind reader, Mr. Sykes." Salverton stiffened to hear his coachman promoted to *Mr.* Sykes.

Sykes peered through the shadows at her. "I know a romantic lady when I see her. I'm a bit inclined that way myself." He lifted his hat and smiled.

"Thank you, Sykes. You may proceed," Salverton said in a stiff voice.

Sykes returned his hat to his head and resumed his place on the box. As the carriage moved forward, Salverton turned a grim face to Samantha.

"It may be the custom for a servant to treat his employers as equals in Milford, Miss Oakleigh. In London, it is not the thing."

"Sykes is not the usual sort of servant. He worked as a secretary for Lord Egremont, so he must be educated. He seems quite gentlemanly."

Salverton made no claims to mind reading, but he knew instinctively it was not any gentlemanly quality on the counter jumper's part that had caught Samantha's interest. It was his bold, handsome face and flirtatious manner.

"He's a forward fellow. Give him an inch and he'll take a mile. He'll be asking if he may call on you if you go on treating him as an equal."

"I doubt he would drive all the way to Milford to call on me. Sykes is the sort who would have a string of girls in Brighton. Oh! There is the sea now, just as he said. How beautiful it is."

Salverton was not the romantic sort who had ever taken much aesthetic interest in the sea. When he was a boy, he wanted to be a pirate. As a grown man, his interest in the sea was limited to storms that might ravage shipping or troops on their way to Spain. He looked at the sea now, and was struck at its beauty. The fat white moon cast a net of sparkling ripples on the black surface. He wouldn't have been much surprised to see a mermaid emerge and flaunt her long tresses at the moon. One lone ship was scudding toward Brighton. Its white sails looked ghostly in the moonlight.

"Wouldn't you love to be on that ship," Samantha said in a softly yearning voice.

He looked at her, and saw the air of enchantment she wore. "I know a romantic lady when I see one," Sykes had said. How had Salverton not sensed that streak in her? He had looked and seen only a provincial greenhead who was too outspoken for propriety. He hadn't seen the provincial whose one trip to London had been spoiled by a foolish brother. If she had come to him when she arrived, he could have given her a romantic visit to remember for a lifetime.

When he asked her why she hadn't come to him sooner, she had said she came to have fun, so she hadn't bothered him. There was a facer! Was that how his relatives saw him—an object of overweening ambition, too busy to enjoy life? Worse—were they right? He usually spent a few weeks in Brighton every summer, but he had never before stopped to admire the moonlight on the water.

He suddenly wanted to talk to Samantha, to tell her he was not so averse to fun as she thought. But it was clear she was in no mood for conversation. She just sat gazing at that moon with such a wistful expression on her pretty face. It couldn't be just the moon and the water. Only a love affair could cause that rapturous look. Who was she picturing on the boat with her? She said she didn't have a beau.

After a mile of silence, the carriage drew to a stop at a gatepost. "The Laurels" was written in wrought iron in an arch spanning the stone gateposts. In the near distance behind the gate, a few lights could be seen between the swaying branches of trees that lined either side of the drive.

Sykes dismounted and decided to open the carriage door for the young lady. "Is the lad likely to do a flit if he hears us coming?" he asked Salverton.

"He might if he thinks it is Sir Geoffrey," Samantha said to Salverton.

"I'll draw the rig under the trees and we'll go ahead on foot," Sykes said.

"You may remain with the carriage, Sykes,"

Salverton said. "You come with me, Samantha." He offered her his arm. He hadn't meant to call her Samantha. It was Sykes's forward behavior that caused this need to display his closer relationship with her. Was he really sunk to competing with that jackanapes?

She linked her arm through his, smiled at Sykes, and she and Salverton began the walk up the roadway to The Laurels. Dark trees whispered on either side as the wind breathed quietly. In the distance, the lapping of water on the shingle beach echoed softly. The tang of salt and seaweed hung on the air. Salverton noticed none of this romantic atmosphere.

"When did you tell Sykes why we're here?" he asked.

"At Winkler's. Why? Should I not have done so?"

"I had some hope we might keep this excursion quiet."

"Oh, is that all you're worried about? I told Mr. Sykes it was a private matter. He won't tell anyone," she said unconcernedly.

"You put a deal of faith in a perfect stranger."

She just shook her head at his jaundiced view of mankind.

As Sykes had said, the house was a little thatched cottage, done in the half-timbered style of the Tudors, and appeared to be of that ancient age. The place had a derelict air. Dust dulled the windows and the grass had grown long. Climbing roses had lost their grip and tumbled to the ground, where roses bloomed in profusion, filling the night with their cloying sweetness. No lights showed below stairs, but on the top floor two curtained windows emitted a dull glow.

"At least they're sleeping in separate bedrooms," Samantha said.

Salverton made no reply to this. He thought Darren an even greater fool if he was not even enjoying the woman's favors after all his scampering about on her behalf.

"We'll frighten them to death if we knock on the door at this hour," Samantha said.

"What are you suggesting—that we break in, or go away after coming so far?"

"No, we cannot leave." She stepped up to the door and tapped timidly. The door knocker had been removed to prevent theft.

Salverton reached over her shoulder and delivered a much harder knock. They waited and repeated the knocking three more times.

"By God, I'll kick the door in," Salverton said, his ire rising at this shabby treatment.

"Allow me," a voice at his shoulder said. It was Sykes.

"I told you to stay with the carriage," Salverton barked.

"It's safe as a babe in its mama's arms. I drew into the roadway, just inside the gate. I thought you might need a strong arm."

Salverton considered his own arm, or more probably his foot, quite capable of battering down the door.

"I'll just open the door for you," Sykes said, and drew out a ring of keys. He fingered them a moment while examining the lock. Then he selected one and inserted it. After a couple of jiggles the door opened.

"After you, Miss Oakleigh," he said, ushering her in.

"The fellow's a ken smasher," Salverton said in a low voice to Samantha as he followed her in.

Sykes overheard and replied. "No such a thing, milord. I only use my *passe-partout* in cases of necessity."

They all went into the dark hallway. Samantha called up the stairs, "Darren! It's Samantha. Come down."

Salverton took one step after her and immediately received a blow on the head from a poker. It was administered by a servant in his nightshirt. It didn't fell Salverton, but it hurt like the devil. A shower of red stars danced before his eyes. A string of expletives flew unbidden from his lips.

Before he could retaliate for the blow, a small, gray-haired gentleman in a silk dressing gown stepped out from the shadow, leveling a pistol at him. To complete the welcoming party, an elderly lady with an ordinary blue pelisse thrown over her nightgown and with her hair done up in papers advanced, wielding a riding crop.

"Send to Rottingdean for a constable, Gratton," the man said to his footman. "Martha, get some ropes to tie them up. What is the world coming to, gangs of thieves and thugs breaking into a gentleman's house!"

Visions of court, a scandal, losing his promotion and his bride reeled in Salverton's head. He had never in his life been involved in anything so déclassé, and for it to happen at this time seemed extraordinarily perverse of fate. He was determined to keep his identity a secret at all costs. He'd pay the fine and hopefully escape with his reputation intact.

Martha lit a candle, the better to see the intruders.

"I'm so very sorry!" Samantha said, advancing to the gentleman. "This is a dreadful mistake. We thought my brother was here."

The lady of the house mistrusted that fond smile that seized her husband's face when he beheld Samantha. "A doxie!" she said in disgust. "You should be ashamed of yourself, miss."

Sykes shouldered his way to the front of the group. "See here, my good lady, this is Lord Salverton and his friend what you're deeneegrating."

Martha held the lamp in Salverton's direction and gasped. "Good God! So it is. Harold, this is Lord Salverton! Milord, I'm so sorry. But what are you doing here?"

Salverton recognized the woman then. She looked quite different with her hair screwed up in papers. He was more accustomed to seeing her in a feathered bonnet in assorted saloons. It was Mrs. Abercrombie, a bishop's niece who had a precarious foothold in the homes of the great. Salverton cast a look of loathing on Jonathon Sykes.

"Mrs. Abercrombie," he said, and bowed punctiliously while he rifled his mind for an acceptable excuse for breaking into her house in the middle of the night.

Chapter Five

Mrs. Abercrombie subjected Samantha to a hard stare that concentrated on her bonnet. "Who is your friend, Lord Salverton?" she asked.

"My cousin," he said without giving a name.

Samantha, eager to ingratiate herself, stepped forward and curtsied. "Miss Oakleigh, from Drumquin, near Bath," she said.

Mrs. Abercrombie made a careful note of the accent—provincial but decidedly ladylike. But then, no lady would be caught dead in that bonnet. "And are you on your way to London, Miss Oakleigh?" she asked.

"To Bath, from London," Salverton replied. "A death in the family. Miss Oakleigh's aunt passed away."

"Who would that be, milord? Surely not your aunt, Lady Edith Blythe? I hadn't heard she was ill."

"Not *my* aunt, Mrs. Abercrombie. My *cousin's*. I doubt you would know her."

"But Brighton is hardly on the way from London to Bath."

"I had planned only to deliver Miss Oakleigh to her—godfather," he said, clutching at straws.

"Harold, pour his lordship a glass of wine while I

slip upstairs and put something on," Mrs. Abercrombie said. She was thrilled to death to have Salverton at her mercy, and determined to discover all the interesting details of this nocturnal visit.

Salverton was equally determined to thwart her. To forestall further questioning as to why he had chosen this cottage, he said, "You are too kind, ma'am, but we wouldn't dream of disturbing you further. We were under the misapprehension that this was Sir Geoffrey Bayne's cottage."

"It is! We hired it from him for the summer. Our son, Peter, made the arrangement for us. The place has gone to rack and ruin. The gardens—but it's impossible to hire a decent place in Brighton. I insisted I must get away from London. This is the best we could do. So Sir Geoffrey is Miss Oakleigh's godfather, you say. I had no idea he was a friend of yours, Lord Salverton."

"We are not close, as you may have guessed from my thinking he was holidaying here."

"Is Miss Oakleigh actually related to Sir Geoffrey?" the lady persisted.

"Connected," Salverton said. He reached to shake Mr. Abercrombie's hand, bowed to the lady, and exited on a series of apologies for having disturbed them, and apologies from Mrs. Abercrombie for having coshed him.

"Well, that was a fine how-do-you-do!" Salverton exclaimed in disgust when they were safely outside.

"You were wonderful, Cousin!" Samantha exclaimed, and reached up to plant a quick kiss on his cheek. "Thank you for leaving Darren out of it."

His look of surprise was for the unexpected kiss. Samantha misinterpreted it. "Oh, that's not why you did it—to protect Darren, I mean. How foolish of me," she said, her admiration fading. "It was Louise you were thinking of. But surely she would understand your helping a cousin."

"Not in this manner. And not such a pretty female cousin."

They began the walk down the road to the carriage. Jonathon Sykes kept pace at Samantha's other side.

"Jealous, is she? If worse comes to worst, you could introduce us," she said. "Then she'll see I'm harmless."

Glancing at Samantha's mobile face in the moonlight, Salverton didn't think Lady Louise would understand at all.

Sykes said in a conspiratorial manner to Samantha, "Ladies never understand when their beau goes out of his way to help a lady prettier than themselves, Miss Oakleigh."

"You don't know I'm prettier than Lady Louise, Mr. Sykes," she replied with an arch smile that infuriated her cousin.

"If Lady Louise was as pretty as you, ma'am—no offense melord—the whole world would be talking of her," was his bold reply. Samantha's smile led him on to greater heights. "Bonnets would be named in her honor, her face would decorate shop windows, ballads would be composed."

Salverton released his ire by saying, "It wasn't necessary for you to tell the Abercrombies my name, Sykes. They didn't appear to recognize me at first."

"They would have afore the constable arrived."

"You know that is true, Cousin," Samantha said. "And I must say, it certainly turned the tide in our favor. She even apologized for having her servant hit you with the poker. Does it hurt?" she remembered to ask.

He fingered his forehead. "Yes, very much."

"I shall put something on it when we get to— Where are we going from here?"

"We'll try the inns in Brighton."

Sykes cleared his throat. "Miss Oakleigh must be fagged. The ladies haven't our stamina, melord. They're delicate flowers. It'll be getting pretty late before we're back at Brighton. Why not call off the chase until morning? If you'll give me the description of Miss Oakleigh's brother and his bit o' muslin, I'll have a run around town for you. If they're in Brighton, Jonathon Sykes will find them, never you fear."

"What do you say, Samantha?" Salverton said. He didn't notice that he had called his cousin by her name this time. His mind was fully occupied in conjuring with the recklessness of visiting some inn overnight with Samantha, *sans* chaperon. Samantha noticed it, and wondered if that blow had done more damage than he realized.

"That is very kind of Mr. Sykes," she said with a smile at their benefactor. "I am tired. Auntie and I were up at the crack of dawn preparing for our trip, you know. To say nothing of being up half the night waiting for Darren to come home. Actually, I didn't sleep at all."

"Then you shall sleep now, and I'll find Darren," Sykes announced.

Salverton was in the position of having either to take orders from his servant or appear a monster by insisting that Samantha continue searching that night.

"Take us back to Brighton," he said to Sykes. "I shall think about it while we go."

Sykes gave Samantha a commiserating glance. Before hopping up on the perch, he went into the road and looked up and down.

"It is no matter if we're seen," Salverton told him. "Mrs. Abercrombie will soon spread the gossip."

"I was wondering if that rider who followed us from Brighton is still on our tail," Sykes replied.

"What rider!" Salverton exclaimed.

"We picked him up at the detour. Likely he was after us before that, but the road out of Brighton was busy. I didn't notice him until we turned off the main road. I blame myself entirely for not noticing him and taking evasive action. You'd expect a mounted rider to pass an old rig like this, but he never did. When I sped up, he sped up. When I slowed down, he slowed down. He was following us right enough."

"Who could he be?" Samantha asked in confusion. "Surely not Sir Geoffrey, hoping to find Wanda by following us?"

"That's possible," Salverton said. "Keep an eye out, Sykes. If you see him again, stop. I'd like a word with Bayne."

"It was never Bayne," Sykes said with great certainty. "Bayne never rides. He's too fleshy and too lazy."

Salverton shrugged his shoulders and assisted Samantha into the carriage, away from Sykes's big ears. "Sykes's mysterious rider was probably a stray traveler afraid to pass this derelict carriage in case we robbed him," he said.

"Highwaymen are usually mounted, not riding in

a carriage. I wonder if *he* was a highwayman! How exciting!" Salverton gave her a damping glare and watched as her smile faded. "Why do you want to speak to Sir Geoffrey?" she asked.

"I am hoping that if we repay his thousand pounds, he'll withdraw his charge."

"Darren doesn't have the money—in cash, I mean."

"I realize that. I'll lend it to him."

"Oh, would you, Cousin? How kind you are! Naturally he'd repay you with interest."

"So I would hope," Salverton said, and again watched the smile fade from her face. Now, why the devil had he said that? He wasn't worried about the money. "It's worth a good deal more than a thousand to me to avoid the scandal," he added, which hardly helped matters.

"I'm afraid we've been a horrid nuisance."

"It's not unusual for provincials to be taken advantage of on their first foray into the city. I'm happy you came to me, Samantha, however belatedly."

"I wager you were never taken advantage of, Cousin."

A rueful smile softened his harsh features. "Now, there you are very much mistaken," he said in a voice of fond remembrance. It was a tone Samantha had not heard him use before.

"No, really? Tell me about it."

Salverton hesitated only a moment before speaking. He had never told anyone of his disgrace. He had managed to forget it for a decade, but he found the memory was still green. The affair with Esmée Labelle had taught him a lesson he had never forgotten. Perhaps he had become too cautious, but it was a close-run thing.

"Her name was Esmée," he said softly. "She was a minor actress at Covent Garden. I saw her on the stage and went to the greenroom after to meet her. I had just finished university that spring, and thought I was cock of the walk. She became my mistress. I hired her a little cottage in St. John's Wood, where I set her up and showered her with knickknacks. One night she and her cohort fed me doctored wine. I was unconscious for twenty-four hours. When I came to, she handed me a wedding license indicating we had been married the day before."

"Her cohort? You mean she had another fellow on the string all the time?"

"He was her older brother, as it turned out. I still hold him responsible. Esmée wasn't clever enough, or wicked enough, to invent such a scheme by herself. I was petrified that they'd show the license to Papa, and paid them whatever they demanded to keep it quiet. They held me to ransom for that whole season. My papa thought I had taken to gambling. That spree went a long way toward killing my father. In desperation I finally went to my cousin Aldred Blythe, a man-about-town, and asked if there was anything I could do short of murdering the pair of them. Even that occurred to me.

"Aldred nearly split his sides laughing. That stunt was as well known as an old ballad. It turned out there was no Mr. Spickleton, the vicar who was supposed to have married us, and no church called St. Peter's-by-the-Woods. They had gotten hold of a forged wedding license. I wanted to forget the whole thing, rack it up to experience, but in the end I felt I owed it to society to expose them. I reported them to Bow Street, and appeared in court to give evidence. Society had me branded as not only a lecher, but a fool. Of course I never recovered the three thousand pounds they had gotten from me, but I've made a point to recover my reputation."

"Was that when you became so—"

"When I acquired my overweening ambition?" he asked in a thin voice.

"And your overweening propriety," she added, softening the words with a saucy smile.

"I expect it is. I certainly wanted to show Papa I wasn't the wastrel he thought me. I did take up my seat in the House at that time, and limited my acquaintances to decent, respectable folks. No one has called me Lord Salty since then."

"I hope Darren's experience has a similar effect. You have certainly lived down your disgrace. I never even heard that story."

"I managed to keep it out of the journals, but it was whispered behind raised hands in society."

Samantha studied her cousin in the moonlight. "I cannot imagine you chasing after an actress. She must have been lovely." As she gazed at his face, softened by memory, she saw the echo of a younger, more dashing Edward, and wished she had known him.

"I thought so, at the ripe old age of one and twenty. As a matter of fact, I still think so," he said musingly. "Esmée had titian hair and green eyes. She was a lively little thing."

"I feel I know you better after hearing your story, Cousin," Samantha said.

Salverton took her hand, squeezed her fingers, and immediately released them. "Well enough to call me Edward, I think."

"It was only seven or eight hours ago you pokered up when I called you that. I think this horrid escapade of Darren's has done you some good."

"Perhaps you're right. Recalling my flaming youth, now that I am older, I find I can forgive myself."

"Good gracious! Has it taken you ten years to forgive yourself? I would have thought a hair shirt would wear out long before that."

"So it should, but when you train an animal harshly, he stays trained after the whip is abandoned."

"Poor Salverton," Samantha said, patting his hand.

"Poor Samantha, saddled with a tartar for a helper."

"You're not such a tartar," she said forgivingly.

Having exhausted this topic, she turned to admire the sea before it disappeared from view. She thought about Esmée, and a young Edward.

"It is hard to think of you being in love," she said.

He stiffened up. "If you're implying I'm marrying Louise only because her papa is in the Cabinet, you are greatly mistaken."

"In a cabinet? Is he a loony? Oh, you mean *the* Cabinet, at Whitehall. Of course. Actually I was speaking of Esmée—thinking of her, you know, so the Cabinet did not come to mind."

"I expect Esmée was an infatuation," he said, embarrassed for his outburst. "I recovered, eventually. My feelings for Louise are quite different. She is a much more serious lady, takes a keen interest in politics."

This hardly reeked of romance, or even love. "Papa had no opinion of politics. He said it was merely the legalized picking of the farmers' pockets by the chosen few."

"It costs money to run a country," he said.

"And pay for Prinny's extravagances."

"That, too. I pay my share, and resent every penny of it."

They reached Brighton within the twenty minutes stipulated by Sykes. It seemed impossible to Samantha that she and Salverton were getting on so well, after she had subjected him to such humiliation. He was beginning to seem quite human. With the proper wife, he would recover from his stiff ways. But Lady Louise, she felt, was not the lady to complete the necessary change. If only she had a little more time to work on him.

Salverton saw her frown and said, "We're here. Don't worry, Samantha. It will soon be over."

"Yes," she said, attempting a wan smile. That was what she was afraid of.

Chapter Six

Sykes drew the team to a smooth halt at the east end of Marine Parade and descended to speak to Lord Salverton.

"Which hotel do you want to go to, melord?" he asked. "Not one of the fancier ones, eh, when your errand is of a clandestine nature?"

Salverton cast a troubled glance at Samantha. It seemed wrong to take his cousin to a lower-class establishment, yet Sykes was right about the secrecy, damn his eyes.

"No doubt you can recommend one that is clean and decent but not well known, Mr. Sykes," Samantha suggested.

It annoyed Salverton that she called him "Mr. Sykes." He was a servant; he was Sykes. And furthermore, he disliked that Sykes called himself, Salverton, "melord." Servants generally called their master "your lordship." Even a simple "sir" was preferable to "melord." That had a touch of familiarity to it. He wished for no familiarity beyond the necessary with the jackanapes Sykes.

In a fit of pique, Salverton said, "We will go to the Curzon, Sykes." The Curzon was in the heart of polite Brighton, just at the north end of Cavendish Place.

"You'll meet half of polite London there," Sykes warned him.

"Let us go to some smaller establishment, Edward," Samantha urged.

"I've already asked my groom to meet us at the Curzon at eight in the morning."

"I could leave a message for Foley," Sykes suggested.

Objection had the effect of hardening Salverton's resolution. "The Curzon, Sykes," he said firmly.

"You're paying the piper; you call the tune," Sykes said doubtfully, and returned to his perch to wheel them along to the elegant Curzon Hotel.

At one A.M., parties were ending; the hotel was bristling with people. Salverton recognized several of them, who would just as quickly recognize him if he descended from the carriage. When he spotted Lady Louise's friend, Miss Hanson, among the throng, he was ready to change his mind—until Sykes's face appeared at the window.

"I don't like to say I told you so," he said with a saucy grin. "Shall I go on to the Brighton Arms, melord?"

"This will do fine, thank you," Salverton said, and alit.

Having bit off his own nose to spite his face, he at least retained enough sense to see if rooms were available before assisting Samantha from the carriage. By ducking and dodging he managed to avoid Miss Hanson, and was vastly relieved to be told there were no rooms available.

He could say with an easy conscience when he returned to the carriage, "They're all filled up. All the better hotels will be at the end of May. We'll try the place you recommended, Sykes."

The carriage proceeded smoothly north to a street one block long called Stone Street. It was respectable if not elegant. The Brighton Arms was a private residence that had been turned into a rooming house. It had a small tavern-cum-coffee shop on the ground floor. A sign in the window advertised "Vacancies," but the house was in darkness. Sykes hopped down and opened the carriage door for them.

"The place is closed for the night," Samantha pointed out.

"That's all right. I'll set you up with Mabel," Sykes said. "My old aunt Mabel Sykes runs the place for me. I'll see you get a good price, melord."

"You mean you own the establishment!" Samantha said approvingly, as if the ramshackle house were the prestigious Pulteney, or Clarendon.

"I won it in a game of cards," Sykes boasted.

Salverton reminded himself never to play cards with Sykes as he took his cousin's arm to lead her up the cobblestone walk.

Sykes pulled his enormous key ring out of his pocket and unlocked the door. With a flourishing bow he bade them enter. Inside, he lit a lamp and led them to a deal table and hard-backed chair that served as a registration desk at the bottom of the front stairs.

Samantha looked around at a wainscoted hallway with aging flowered paper above. The oak floor was badly warped, but it was not so very dusty. The air was chill and smelled moldy.

"You can use any name you like," Sykes said, pushing the registry toward them. "I mostly get gents named Mr. Smith or Jones. I'll tell Mabel you're friends of mine. That'll be a guinea each for the two rooms, and another if you want hot water and breakfast in the morning."

Salverton felt two guineas would have set them up in better style at the Curzon, but he was too fatigued and restive to argue. He placed two guineas on the desk. They promptly disappeared into Sykes's pocket, where they rattled merrily against his keys.

Below a list of anonymous Mr. Smiths, Salverton wrote Mr. Jones, London. Samantha looked at it and wrote Miss Smith, London, below.

"I feel like a criminal," she said, laughing.

"What you need is a nice cup of tea," Sykes said. "I'll fetch Mabel, then have a quick scour of the inns for your brother and his woman. What is the lass's name?"

"Wanda Claridge," Samantha said.

"Wanda Claridge? That's odd. Bayne's been seen about with Nancy Hewitt the last months. Is she a dark-haired beauty?"

"That's her. She's calling herself Wanda Claridge this month," Samantha said.

"I first knew her as Sally Bright. Now, what has she been up to that she's gone and changed her name again?"

"She's robbed Sir Geoffrey of a thousand pounds."

"She's a live one is Nancy," said Sykes approvingly, "but we'll catch her."

"Thank you, Mr. Sykes. I don't know what we would have done without you," she said.

Sykes left. Salverton took two steps that led to the archway into the main saloon. He was not pleased but he was not surprised either to see a man in a fustian jacket and stocking feet stretched out on a sofa, snoring.

"Make sure you lock your door before retiring," he said to Samantha.

She looked over his shoulder at the sleeper and shook her head. "I wager you have not been in a place like this since you were seeing Esmée, Edward."

"I had hoped I never would be again," he replied, but he said it with a wry chuckle.

Mabel Sykes soon appeared. The dumpy woman with gray hair scrunched into a knob at the back of her head bore no resemblance to her nephew. Her face looked like a lump of leavened dough with two peeled grapes for eyes.

"This way," she said, stifling a yawn, and led them upstairs.

The rooms were numbered, not named. "Numbers three and five are the only vacancies. There's a connecting door between them," she added, obviously assuming the two rooms were a mere camouflage for debauchery.

"Do you have a key for the connecting door?" Salverton inquired stiffly.

"Oh, no, sir. She can't lock herself in," she said with a roguish shake of her head.

Salverton thought it better not to pursue this line. Samantha was shown into her room first. Mabel lit a lamp, which cast a wan beam on a small chamber with a canted roof, unadorned walls distempered in yellow, a quilted double bed with no canopy, a plain wooden floor, and a table holding a water pitcher and basin. Mabel led Salverton along to a similar room done in blue. She said, "Good luck, mister," and vanished quietly.

Salverton thought he ought to apologize to Samantha for the shabby room. Knowing she hadn't had time to undress, he tapped lightly at the connecting door. It opened at once, and a tousle of blond curls appeared.

"I was wondering if I should say good night to you," she said.

She still wore her pelisse. With her bonnet removed, she looked more ladylike, and completely out of place in her surroundings.

"Perhaps we should leave," he said uncertainly. "There might be one room for you at least at Brunswick Terrace or the Bedford."

"The rooms are quite clean," she said. She looked so weary that he didn't push the matter. "It's only for one night. Do you mind terribly, Edward? I know it is not at all what you are accustomed to, but if you could view it as an adventure—"

"I'm not thinking of myself!"

"You need not worry about me. I would like nothing better than to fall into that bed and sleep the clock around."

"As you say, it's only for one night. We'll want an early start in the morning. We're to meet Foley at eight. I'll have him take us someplace decent for breakfast."

"You've already paid for breakfast here."

"That was before I saw the rooms."

"Let us eat here before meeting Foley. It will save time, and no one will see us."

"Those are two important considerations. Very well. Good night, Samantha. Don't worry. We'll find Darren."

"Oh, yes, I have every reliance that Mr. Sykes will find him at one of the hotels. Good night, Edward."

On this facer, she closed the door. Salverton felt

an angry clenching in his chest. Mr. Sykes would find him! There was gratitude for you! He wanted a glass of wine and a cheroot, neither of which was available to him at the moment. He hadn't brought a change of clothes. He'd have to put on a used shirt tomorrow morning and borrow Sykes's razor. And meanwhile his report for Liverpool sat unfinished on his desk. When would he have time to finish it?

He had handled this whole affair badly. He ought to have come to Brighton by himself and left Samantha at home with her aunt. Yet he knew the trip would not have been half so exciting without her. It was being with a lady that lent the proceedings the air of an escapade.

He undressed and got into bed. The sheets were clean so far as he could tell. The feather tick and pillow formed a cloud of softness beneath him. He was about to doze off, when he heard some sound from Samantha's room. He was instantly out of bed, feeling in the darkness for his trousers.

When she closed the door on Salverton, Samantha found she was really remarkably hungry, despite a good dinner. Mr. Sykes had said he would get her tea. Had he remembered? She delayed undressing in hopes that he would. Barring the tea, she remembered a small bag of lemon drops in her reticule. Not very satisfying, but better than nothing. She popped one into her mouth.

Sykes's tap at the door was so soft, she hardly heard it. She tiptoed forward to avoid disturbing Edward, next door. There stood Mr. Sykes with a tray holding not only a teapot, but two cups, a plate of bread and butter, and a nice wedge of Stilton cheese.

"How lovely!" she said softly, and stood aside while he brought the tray in.

"I brought two cups, in case him next door would like to join you."

"Oh, I don't think so. He's gone to bed. At least I heard the bed squawk." Mr. Sykes was looking a question at her. "Perhaps you would like to join me, Mr. Sykes?" she suggested.

"I don't mind if I do," he said. "Just a quick cup before starting my rounds of the hotels."

"We're keeping you up very late."

"Nay, five or six is late. Any time before Mr. Cock crows is early."

As there were no chairs, she poured the two cups of tea and they took them standing up.

Sykes sipped noisily, then said, "Did you know Wanda has a daughter?"

"No! I didn't know she'd been married. In that case, at least she cannot get Darren to the altar."

"She never was married so far as I know. A by-blow, not Sir Geoffrey's. The girl is called Amy Bright."

"Wanda never said a word about her. Of course she could hardly tell us, when she was posing as a respectable lady."

"You're too green by half, my girl. Wanda's no lady, and neither is Amy."

"What age is Amy?"

"Fifteen, and already hard at work."

"Poor child. What does she do?"

"She's following the family profession, isn't she? Amy's a hostess at Mike Skelton's gaming hell, over on Queen's Road, when she isn't otherwise occupied. What I was thinking—Amy might know where her mama is."

"We should ask her!"

"Aye, we should. It could save a deal of scrambling about town. Grab your pretty bonnet and let's go."

Samantha looked uncertainly at the connecting door to Salverton's room. No, she wouldn't ask him to go along. It did occur to her, however, that Mr. Sykes might go alone. She suggested it to him.

"My first thought was to spare you, Miss Oakleigh," he said, gazing at her from a pair of eyes as beautiful and unfeeling as star sapphires. "The devil of it is, a fellow isn't allowed into Mike's place without a lady. It's for couples only. The ladies feel uncomfortable with too many men leering over their shoulders. It's a decent sort of place. I'll see no harm comes to you."

"Thank you, Mr. Sykes," she said, and picked up her bonnet and pelisse. Sykes smiled appreciatively while she put on the former, and helped her on with the latter. Of course he had lied about the necessity of Samantha's accompanying him, but he meant her no harm. He did it as much to goad that toplofty Salverton as anything.

Before they left, he picked up two slices of bread and butter, wrapped each one around a wedge of cheese, and handed her one. "No point wasting good food," he said. Samantha agreed, and was happy he had thought of it.

Salverton had realized by this time that Samantha was speaking to someone in her room. He could hear movement and the low hum of voices. He assumed it was Mabel. There had been some mention of tea, but on the off chance that that jackanapes of a Sykes had inveigled his way into her room, he hastened his dressing.

His knock at the door brought no response. He opened it and looked into a perfectly empty room. In her eagerness to leave, she hadn't even extinguished her lamp. He saw the teapot and food on the washstand. He saw the two used cups, and knew Samantha had not crept out into the night alone, or with Mabel Sykes. She was with that scoundrel! When he found them, he would wring both their necks. But first he had to find them—and it was four pence to a groat that Sykes had taken the carriage.

Chapter Seven

Salverton snatched up his jacket and hat on the run. He pelted into the road just as the carriage turned the corner to Castle Street. He ran after it, shouting, and managed to keep it in sight to the next corner, where it turned east on the Western Road. Sykes would take the Dyke Road north, out of town. The bastard was kidnapping Samantha! Salverton was gasping for breath from running, and all the while the carriage was drawing farther away from him. He cursed himself for having taken her to Sykes's lair.

He'd have to report it to the constable. Bow Street would be called in at once. Strangely, it was not the shame and disgrace of it that bothered Salverton, but the realization that Samantha was in danger. Why the devil hadn't she called out for help? She knew he was right next door.

He paused a moment and stood, rubbing his chin. The answer was staring him in the face. Samantha hadn't been kidnapped. The baggage had gone off willingly with her Mr. Sykes, not realizing what a villain the man was. The thing to discover was where Sykes was taking her. At best, it would be to some déclassé party or gaming hell. That would be the lure he held out to get her away from the house in any case.

Mabel would know his usual haunts. Salverton walked quickly back to the lodging house on Stone Street, in the front door, down the hallway, down a flight of stairs to the kitchen area, from which Mabel had appeared. He called loudly as he went.

Mabel Sykes came scrambling out of a room off the kitchen.

" 'Ere!" she exclaimed. "What's going on, mister? Why are you shouting to wake the dead? We got paying guests to think of." In her right hand she had a firm grasp on a butcher knife, which she kept under her pillow at night.

"Where's Sykes?" Salverton demanded.

"He was taking tea up to you and your piece, the last I seen of him."

"He's gone off in my carriage with my cousin. Where would he be taking her?"

"Lord love me, is that all? I thought you was robbed, at least. Now, how should I know where they've gone to? Jon is friends with every rake and rattle in town. It's the touch of quality that gets to him every time, mister. Your bit o' muslin was very ladylike, for one of them. He's very partic'lar in his flirts, is Jonathon. How did she get away on you? You've hardly had time—"

"I have reason to believe your nephew used some stunt to get my cousin to go with him. Where is he?"

"You can ask till the cows come home, mister, and neither you nor me nor the doorknob will be any the wiser. I don't know where he's gone, and that's a fact. I ain't his wife or his ma. He's a grown man. He does what he likes. But I'll tell you this, you needn't fear for her safety, one way or t'other. Jon don't have to force them. He treats a lady proper. Just go on back to bed, and if she's a mind to, she'll be back waiting for you by morning."

On this speech she turned to leave. After taking one step, she turned to look back over her shoulder. "You wasn't fool enough to pay him in advance, by chance?"

"He's been well rewarded," Salverton replied, stinging from that thoughtless and well-deserved "fool."

"Well then, he's gone to a gaming hell, hasn't he? Try Mrs. Nesbitt's on Golden Lane, or Meg— No, he'd not take a lady there. He could be at Mrs. Minchin's."

"He headed north up the Dyke Road."

"The Dyke Road, you say? That'd be Mike Skelton's place, then. Odd he'd take her there. There's no shortage of lightskirts at Mike's place."

Salverton fumed in silent rage. "Where is it?"

"On the Dyke Road, just north of the cemetery."

"Is there a mount here I can ride?" Mabel's gooseberry eyes emitted a curious gleam, half fear, half greed. Salverton drew out his purse and extracted a golden boy. "It's urgent," he said, fingering the coin enticingly.

Mabel reached out and snatched it from his fingers. "Caesar. A gray gelding hitched to the tree in the backyard. Gelding hasn't tamed the brute much. Mind you have it back before morning or Jon'll have my head on a platter like the martyr I am."

Salverton didn't reply, but pelted out the door and around to the backyard. He heard a whicker and followed it to a spreading mulberry, where he discovered a well-groomed gray, instead of the tired jade with a spavined back he expected to see. The saddle hung conveniently nearby on the lower branch of the mulberry tree. After saddling the mount, he had some difficulty convincing Caesar he meant business, but eventually he was in the saddle and on his way north. It took every ounce of his strength to control the powerful animal.

As he entered the Dyke Road, he left polite Brighton behind. Ahead lay a dark, lonesome path. He increased his pace to a gallop. The mount's hooves thundered over the metaled road. A cold moon lent an eerie air to the countryside. Wind stirred the trees that edged the roadside. Beyond the trees lay barren fields and an occasional small dwelling. Salverton regretted he hadn't brought his pistol with him. It was ideal highwayman country. But the big gray set such a fast pace, he doubted anyone could outride him. It was a magnificent mount.

Before long he spotted the spire of a church on his right, and on his left a cemetery. The headstones and monuments shone with a wan and ghastly light. Mike Skelton's gaming hell was not far beyond, according to Mabel. Salverton wasted no time getting past the cemetery, then he slowed to a canter. After half a mile, he spotted a low, spreading house nestled among a bank of sheltering bushes. There was no sign to indicate it was a public establishment, but the number of lit windows suggested it was more than a private residence.

A young stable boy popped out of nowhere. "Can I stable your nag, mister?" he asked. " 'Ere! That's Jon's Caesar, that is."

"What of it? Is Sykes here?" Salverton asked.

"Aye, he just drove his rig 'round to the back hisself. Nipcheese! Too clutch-fisted to pay for a driver, and him with a lady, too."

Salverton flipped the helpful lad a coin. He dismounted and handed him the reins, then strode angrily to the rear of the building. The carriage he had hired was there, empty. The back door of the house was locked, but that, of course, would provide no impediment to Sykes and his passe-partout. Salverton's gorge rose higher as he returned to the front door and walked in without knocking.

A bruiser with shoulders like a clothespress examined him and decided against ejecting him. His pockets looked deep.

"Come for a game of cards, sir?" he asked, smiling and revealing the two or three teeth that remained in his head.

"I'm looking for Sykes," Salverton growled.

The bruiser took one look at Salverton's black scowl and said, "Casino parlor. Upstairs to your left. And no brawling, mind," he called. Salverton had already brushed past him.

He took the uncarpeted stairs two at a time, and soon found himself in a noisy corridor. The two rooms on either side of the hallway were full to overflowing with gamblers of both sexes, none of them respectable, to judge by their appearance. He looked in the closer rooms on either side of the hallway. When he heard the clicking of the roulette wheel and the rattle of dice, he passed on. Casino didn't require either a wheel or dice. He strode on quickly to the next rooms.

It was in the last one that he spotted Sykes. Salverton took one step forward, murder in his heart, and stopped. Samantha wasn't with him. Sykes sat at the casino table, playing cards with three other men. A quick glance around told Salverton that Samantha wasn't in the room. Three of the lower class of lightskirts made up the female contingent.

Salverton hesitated a moment, trying to decide between making a scene and taking a closer look in the other rooms. He was about to leave, when he felt a jiggle on his arm, and a blowsy blonde in an exceedingly low-cut gown leered at him.

"All alone, love?" she asked coyly. "Come and buy me a wee drink. I'll bring you luck. They call me Lucky Lucy."

Salverton recoiled from her touch, and the stench of cheap toilet water that didn't quite succeed in covering even more repugnant odors.

"I'm looking for a young lady," he said to be rid of the harridan.

"Ain't you lucky? You've found me."

"A lady in a blue gown. She came with Jonathon Sykes."

The woman looked Salverton up and down consideringly. "You don't want to tangle with Sykes," she cautioned.

"Did you see her?"

The blonde tossed her head toward a closed door at the end of the hall. "She's with Amy in the ladies' parlor."

"Ladies' parlor?"

"It's all right. Gents are allowed in. It's where they go to pick a girl if they come for something besides gambling," she informed him with another leering smile.

"Oh, Lord!"

Without another word, he rushed to the closed door and threw it open. The ladies' parlor was a large chamber with some pretentions to elegance. It held sofas and saloon furniture, and in one corner, a wine table where a servant was selling wine. A series of doors led off the room. One hung open, showing a bed with a garish red canopy. He checked to see the room was unoccupied before returning his attention to the main room, where he saw a dozen men and girls behaving in a way he considered licentious. Some of the girls were perched on the men's knees. Other men had their arms around the girls' waists. A few tame kisses were being exchanged.

He soon spotted Samantha, sitting on a sofa with another girl much too young to be selling her charms. A man with graying hair took the young girl's arm and led her from the room. She smiled flirtatiously over her shoulder at Salverton as she left. The man at Samantha's side was younger, and rather handsome. He wasn't actually touching her, but he looked as if he'd like to. Salverton's face turned an alarming shade of red.

"Samantha, come here at once!" he exclaimed. Every head in the room turned.

Samantha looked up, and upon seeing Salverton, uttered a strangled gasp, and turned to the man beside her.

"Is he your husband?" the man asked.

"Yes!" Salverton said firmly, figuring that was the easiest way to extricate her.

"Of course not!" she replied simultaneously.

Salverton strode forward and seized Samantha's hand. "You're coming with me, now."

"I told Mr. Sykes I'd meet him here," she replied, wrenching her hand free. "No need for you to remain, Cousin."

He reached out and took her hand again. It was

too much for the man who was with her. He leapt up, bristling.

"The young lady doesn't wish to accompany you, sir."

"You shut your face," Salverton scowled.

"Mr. Sykes will take me home," Samantha said.

"You're coming with me," Salverton insisted.

The altercation drew the attention of the others in the room. A crowd surged forward, sensing a brawl.

The man with Samantha rose and gave Salverton's shoulder a buffet. "The lady says she is not your wife," he said. Salverton ignored the words but returned the buffet. Within seconds, a full-fledged brawl ensued. Without having the least notion who was in the right, the others chose sides and enjoyed a fine battle. Even the women took part. Lacking strength to deliver a telling blow, they availed themselves of vases and wine bottles.

When Samantha saw that Salverton was being attacked by two men at once, she grabbed up one of the wine bottles and lowered it over the head of one of them.

"Salverton, you *idiot*!" she said, and was rewarded with a murderous scowl.

"There's gratitude for you!" he growled.

Neither of them noticed the female behind Salverton as she lifted a sturdy china jug and lowered it with considerable force over Salverton's head. Samantha heard a menacing thump as it came in contact with his skull. Salverton cast a darkly accusing eye at her as he fell to the floor.

A brace of bruisers came flying in to find the cause of the disturbance, and settle it.

" 'Ere, this is going to cost someone a pretty

penny," a man of mulelike proportions exclaimed. "That's it, folks. Fight's over."

The regulars recognized in the bruiser the proprietor of the establishment, Mike Skelton.

After a little scuffling, the battle dwindled to mere verbal abuse. "He's the one started it," the man who had been protecting Samantha said, pointing at Edward's inert body. He was upheld by others who felt it safe to lay the blame on the unconscious.

Samantha made some effort to revive her protector. When fanning him didn't work, Mike poured a jug of water over his face. Salverton made a gargling sound, but he didn't regain consciousness. Samantha was becoming worried. When she asked for a doctor, Skelton gave her to understand he didn't want the body discovered on his premises.

"I suggest you get him into his carriage and take him to town," he said, but his tone made it a command. "As soon as he's settled up for the damages here, that is to say."

It was all too much for Samantha. "Would you ask Mr. Sykes to join me?" she said. "He's playing casino."

Sykes soon came hastening in. "I thought I heard a racket. I was winning, and didn't care to leave the table. Ah, it's him," he said with a weary glance at the body on the floor. "Is he hurt much?" He bent over Salverton, lifted his eyelids, and announced he was hale and hearty.

"We'll take him home, Miss Oakleigh."

"There's damages!" Skelton said, pointing to the various bits of broken crockery and wine bottles.

Without batting an eyelash, Sykes put his hand into Salverton's jacket and drew out his purse. He took out a couple of bills and handed them to Skelton.

"This'll cover it, Mike, and a little something for your trouble."

Mike's satisfied grin as he left the room told Samantha he'd been generously rewarded.

"Are you sure Salverton is all right?" she asked Sykes when they were alone.

"Just a tap on the head. Did you find out what you wanted to from Amy?"

"Yes. A cottage in Tunbridge Wells."

"Then we'll go back to the hotel."

He hoisted Salverton's inert form over his shoulder as easily as if he were a rag doll and carried him out to the carriage. Samantha rushed to open the carriage door. When Salverton had been stowed within, she hopped in to watch over him.

"Oh, you're riding in there, then, are you?" Sykes said, disappointed. "I thought you'd sit with me on the perch, as you did coming, since you enjoyed it so."

"I'd best keep an eye on him, Mr. Sykes."

"Suit yourself. I wonder how he got here. He wouldn't have borrowed—" He called for the stable boy, who had been watching them.

"That's the bloke as rode your Caesar here," the boy said, pointing to the body in the carriage.

"The devil you say! I didn't think Caesar would let anyone on his back but myself. I'll pick my nag up as soon as I can. Take care of him for me, lad." He tossed the boy tuppence.

"Don't break your thumb, Jon," the boy scowled, but he pocketed the coin.

Sykes hopped onto the perch and the carriage left for the hotel.

Chapter Eight

When Salverton began sliding from the seat, Samantha moved to his banquette and held him in place, with his head in her lap. She wasn't actually worried for Salverton's life. She had seen the china jug that hit him, and didn't think it capable of a fatal blow. What did concern her was what mood he would be in when he regained consciousness.

She brushed the hair from his forehead, noticing how much handsomer he looked when his face was relaxed. It was only his forbidding expression that robbed him of being called handsome. His brow was high and wide, what Mama called a noble brow. She ran her fingers gently over it, feeling the small dents of incipient wrinkles. Then along his high cheekbones, and lower to the hollows of his cheeks. Strange, how you could feel the skeleton bones beneath the flesh. Eerie. She shivered, then traced his nose, a proud, aquiline nose. With one finger she drew the outline of his lips. Nice full lips, when he wasn't pinching them in derision.

Salverton gradually regained consciousness. He thought it must be a dream, those loving fingers caressing him. He was dreaming of Esmée again. He put out his hand and seized the hand that touched him. Then he raised it to his lips and kissed it with a passion that surprised Samantha. He pressed his lips firmly against her palm and held them there a moment.

"That feels good," he murmured in a voice as soft as velvet. Not Salverton's voice at all, but a lover's voice.

Samantha was aware of a strange warmth building inside her as his fingers squeezed hers so intimately. Then she felt exceedingly foolish, as if she'd chanced across her cousin in a state of undress. She cleared her throat.

"It's Samantha, Edward," she said in a matter-of-fact tone. "Are you awake now?"

His head jerked up as if he'd been prodded with a hot poker. She pushed it gently back to her lap.

"It's all right. I know you thought it was Lady Louise. I hope you're not feeling too badly?"

"I didn't think you were Louise. I thought you were—" He rubbed his temples.

"Who? Who did you think I was?" she asked.

"Never mind."

"I shan't tell Louise."

"You won't be meeting her!"

"That's good."

He looked up at the face hovering above him. Her eyes gleamed in the moonlight. He noticed how soft and full her cheeks were. "Why would you not want to meet Louise?" he asked.

"I'm sure I should dislike her excessively. Your voice tightens when you mention her. If *you're* afraid of her, *I* should be terrified."

"Don't be ridiculous! I'm not afraid of her." Yet he did feel a *frisson* to think of her learning of this escapade with Samantha. It made his head ache.

"I feel as if I'd been beaten with cudgels." With a

groan, he sat up and looked out the window. When his head stopped spinning, he said, "Where are we?"

"In your carriage, returning to Brighton."

His face assumed its customary scowl as he turned his thoughts to their situation.

"What the devil were you doing there? Why didn't you tell me? And to go with that jackanapes of a Sykes! Have you no notion of propriety?"

"I have a notion my brother's in trouble!" she shot back. "What do I care what those people thought of me? I went alone with Mr. Sykes because I wanted to spare you," she explained. "I knew it wasn't the sort of place that would amuse you."

"Nor you, I should hope!"

"On the contrary! I was delighted to see what a gaming hell is like. We don't have them in Milford."

"Thank God for that!"

"Oh, Edward!" she scolded. "Don't you ever feel the urge to do something a little outré? I own I've been half envying Darren his escapade with Wanda. Everyone should have one such incident in her life."

"I certainly do not feel anything of the sort."

"Well," she said pensively, "you did when you were young. You've already had your Esmée. I haven't had anything like that. I enjoyed tonight very much. I'm sorry you were hurt, but if you hadn't gone lording it in there like a vengeful Jehovah, demanding I go with you—"

He paused a moment over that thoughtless "when you were young." She made him sound like Methuselah.

"What was I to do?" he asked. "You refused to take my lead and pretend you were my wife."

"As if anyone would believe that!" she scoffed.

"Do you know what kind of a place that is? A house of prostitution, along with a gaming hell. To see that old wretch ogling you as if you were a plum cake!"

"Actually, Mr. Docker was very nice."

"I hope you didn't give him your name!"

"Of course I did. I told him I was Miss Jones, from London. It was his first time there. He's a traveling merchant from Suffolk. He sells cutlery. He was just lonesome. One can understand how it happened—that he went there, I mean. When I told him I wasn't available, he was actually quite relieved! He just wanted to talk."

Salverton shook his head in bewilderment. "I cannot comprehend how a well-raised young lady can be so foolish. Didn't your mama teach you anything?"

"Yes, Edward. She taught me not to be judgmental."

"Well, she shouldn't have!"

A gurgle of laughter was her answer to that. "You are too absurd. In your high state of indignation, you've lost track of why I went there in the first place."

"You've already told me why you went. You wanted a taste of degradation."

"Not at all! That was an added bonus. I went to meet Amy."

"Amy who?" he demanded suspiciously.

"Amy Bright—the chit who was rolling her eyes at you. She's only fifteen, by the bye, so if you have designs—"

"Don't be ridiculous! Who is she?"

"Oh, you don't know. She's Wanda Claridge's daughter."

"Good God! You mean Darren's woman has a grown daughter! She must be old as the hills."

"Well, I don't think she is. When Amy's thirty, she could have a daughter the age she is now. In any case, that's why Jonathon took me there. He knew about Amy."

"Why didn't he tell me? Why did he feel he had to take you along?"

"He said gents weren't allowed in unaccompanied. That was a plumper, of course. Most of them came in alone. What he really wanted was to walk in with a lady on his arm, I think. He cherishes his amorous reputation. All the women there made a great fuss over him."

"Peacock! He shouldn't have taken you—and you shouldn't have gone."

Samantha twinkled a smile at him. "I knew you would feel that way, which is why I didn't tell you I was going. If I hadn't gone, I wouldn't have discovered where Darren and Wanda are. Amy told me."

"Where are they?" he asked eagerly.

"We've been led on a wild-goose chase, Cousin. They didn't come to Brighton at all. I wager Wanda spoke of Brighton so much and had that bathing costume made up only to fool me. There's no bathing at Tunbridge Wells, so far as I know. Amy says Sir Geoffrey has another love nest there. That's where Wanda usually takes her young men, she said. Is it very far away?"

"Halfway between here and London."

"Then perhaps we can stop tomorrow on our way back to London."

"Unfortunately, it's not 'on our way.' It lies well to the east. And I must be in London tomorrow."

"Oh." She looked dejected for a moment, then brightened. "We can ask Mr. Sykes to take me."

Salverton gave a malevolent glare. "Not bloody likely!"

Samantha stared in disbelief. "Gracious, Edward! I never thought I'd hear you say such a thing—and to a lady, too. I do believe you're turning into a human being right before my very eyes." She reached out and gave his chin a saucy squeeze. "Yes, your granite scowl is turning to real flesh and blood. You had best hasten back to Lady Louise, or she'll never recognize you."

"Oh, no, miss, you don't get rid of me that easily. I see what you're about. You want to go scampering off with Sykes to enjoy a further taste of the low life. You will return to London with me, and when I've accomplished my business, we shall go to Tunbridge Wells together. Without Sykes," he added firmly.

"Oh." Her lips pouted in an enchanting *moue*. Salverton gazed, trying in vain to imagine Louise's lips in such an enticing position.

"I think we ought to ask him to come with us, Cousin," she continued. "He's been so very helpful. If it weren't for Mr. Sykes, we wouldn't have found Amy."

"We know where Wanda and Darren are now. We can dispense with Sykes's services," Salverton insisted.

Sykes soon had them back at his rooming house. As they clambered out, he called down to Salverton, "About the blunt missing from your purse, melord, did Miss Oakleigh explain?"

Salverton's eyes narrowed in suspicion. "Miss Oakleigh forgot to mention that. We were having such a delightful conversation, it slipped her mind."

"You had to pay for the damages, see."

Salverton drew out his purse and uttered a light howl of protest. "Ten pounds! Dammit, the only damage was a few broken bits of cheap crockery."

"There was the spillage of wine to the carpets as well," Sykes explained. "Cheap at the price."

"The carpets weren't worth a shilling."

Sykes laughed. "That depends on whether you're buying or selling." He cracked the whip and the carriage moved on.

"Thief," Salverton muttered, counting what remained of his money.

As they went into the house, Samantha asked how his head felt.

"It aches like the deuce. I don't suppose you have any headache powders?"

"I never get headaches," she replied with an apologetic shrug. "I'm disgustingly healthy. Miss Donaldson gets them; she finds a nice cup of tea helps."

"I doubt 'a nice cup of tea' will be available here."

"It's too late to rouse Mr. Sykes's aunt, but if you don't mind taking your tea a little cooled, there's a pot in my room. Mr. Sykes brought it to me," she added with a fond smile.

As Salverton could think of nothing cutting enough to satisfy his fury, he just held the door and glared as she entered.

The tea was at room temperature. The bread had

hardened around the edges as well, but as Samantha poured the tea and urged some refreshment on him, Salverton felt his anger ebb.

No harm had come of the little excursion after all—barring that tap on the head and the loss of ten pounds—and they had gotten a new lead on Darren.

"You wanted a taste of excitement. This will be something to remember when you return to Milford," he said, smiling.

Strangely, now that he had accepted the situation, Samantha was frowning.

"What do you think they'll do to Darren, Edward?" she asked, and gazed at him with such a trusting look that he felt ten feet tall. It had been a long time since a pretty young lady had looked at him like that. He remembered her soft hands caressing his brow.

When he spoke, his voice was gentle. "I'll take care of it, Samantha. Don't worry."

Tears brimmed in her eyes. She brushed them away with the back of her hand. Salverton hadn't quite overcome his aversion to inelegance. He drew out a pristine handkerchief and handed it to her.

"You're so kind," she said, daubing at her tears. "I had no idea you would be so helpful. I didn't want to appeal to you. Miss Donaldson made me. She said you would know what to do, and she was right. It must be difficult, being the one everyone turns to when he's in the suds."

"I do what I can. Family, after all," he said modestly.

"The next time any of our relatives call you stiff-rumped, I shall give them a good piece of my mind," she said.

That brought Salverton back to earth with a thump. "Is that what they say of me behind my back?"

She smiled. "You do give that impression, you know, but I think it's mainly impatience. I'm sure you have all sorts of important things on your mind, a gentleman like you."

"I do carry a heavy load at Whitehall," he admitted, again modestly. "There's a report I should be working on . . . But I shall do as I promised, and look after Darren first."

"Well, you're very kind, Cousin, and I thank you."

She reached up and gave him a kiss on the cheek. For a moment their eyes met and held. Neither of them said anything, but they were both conscious of some emotion more powerful than a simple kiss on the cheek would cause.

After a moment, Salverton cleared his throat. "Happy I could help. Well, good night, Cousin."

"Good night, Edward."

As he returned to his own room, Salverton's fingers massaged the spot where she had kissed him. A small smile tugged at his lips. He wouldn't have admitted it for the world, but he was looking forward to Tunbridge Wells with Samantha, without Jonathon Sykes to cause mischief.

Chapter Nine

Salverton was accustomed to arising at seven to get an early start on his day's work. He disliked dressing in evening clothes in the morning, and especially in yesterday's soiled shirt, but at least he managed to get hot water and the loan of a dull razor from Mabel—for a price. The bump on the back of his head didn't show. As he shaved in the few square inches of dim mirror over his dressing table, however, he noticed that his left eye was bruised from the fight at Mike Skelton's gaming hell. How was he to explain that to Louise? She disapproved of violence, even the socially acceptable sort practiced at Gentleman Jackson's Boxing Parlor.

At half past seven he put his ear to the connecting door to listen for sounds that Samantha was up and dressing. All was silence. The obvious didn't occur to him—that she was still sleeping. He immediately leapt to the conclusion that she had run off to Tunbridge Wells with Sykes—without himself, after all his efforts on her behalf.

He flung the door open and barged into her room. The noise aroused Samantha, who was just awaking. She sat up in her bed, staring in consternation at Salverton. A golden tousle of curls tumbled about her cheeks. Her blue eyes blinked in confusion. Salverton just stared, half in admiration and half in embarrassment. How could a woman look so lovely, so ravishing, so early in the morning?

In the first instant of awakening, Samantha hardly recognized her cousin. Salverton's bruised eye lent him a touch of recklessness. She felt that a strange man was breaking into her room. She pulled the bedcovers up to her chin and emitted one loud, high-pitched scream.

Salverton hastened toward the bed. "Stop that! You'll bring half the house to your door. What's the matter with you?" he demanded, his eyebrows drawn together in a sharp frown.

"Oh, Cousin!" she gasped, and put her fingers to her cheeks in embarrassment as she remembered the night's proceedings. "I'm sorry. You frightened me half to death. I didn't recognize you at first. Is it time to get up?" She reached for her watch that she had placed on the bedside table.

Salverton noticed the becoming lawn nightgown she wore, with rosebuds embroidered by Miss Donaldson across the top. It was far from immodest. More of a lady's body could be seen any night at a polite ball. But it was sleeveless and of a thin material that gave more than a suggestion of the supple curves beneath the gown. He knew he should leave the room, but he just stood, gazing at her as if mesmerized. His eyes moved slowly from her face to her dainty white arms and shoulders, to the thin lawn covering her upper body.

Samantha felt uncomfortable at this close scrutiny. She wasn't afraid of her cousin, but she was shocked at his lack of control. To recall him to propriety, she said, "I had no idea it was so late. If you'll leave, Edward, I shall be dressed and join you in a moment."

He gave her a self-conscious look. "Yes, I'll meet you below," he said, and left the room at a rapid pace, mentally chastizing himself for acting like a Johnnie Raw. But to judge by what he had seen, Samantha's body was enough to make any red-blooded man take a second look. Should he apologize when she joined him? Or would it be best to just ignore that uncomfortable moment?

It occurred to Samantha that Edward had behaved like a schoolboy, or a hungry man looking at a meal. She already suspected the match with Lady Louise was no love match, despite his protests. Did Edward not have a woman on the side? Had his affair with Esmée given him a disgust of hired escorts? What did he do about his physical needs? These thoughts flitted through her mind as she splashed cold water on her face, hastily dressed, and ran a comb through her curls.

At a quarter to eight she joined Salverton. He was waiting for her at the bottom of the staircase.

"We're not eating breakfast here," he said firmly. "I've seen the dining room. It's been taken over by black beetles. Sykes will take the carriage back to Winkler's. We'll walk to the Curzon."

"But you're dressed for the evening. And in that black eye, Edward, you look like a debauched dandy." Her tinkling laughter was not entirely devoid of admiration.

"A case of the pot calling the kettle black," he said, smiling as his gaze moved to her bonnet.

"I doubt they'll let us in the door."

"They've never banned me from entering before. I shouldn't think the hotel will be busy this early in the morning. We'll hire a private parlor and eat there."

A quick glance at the few clients on their way to the breakfast parlor left Samantha with no wish to join them. It would be lovely to sit down at a table with a clean cover and good food.

"We should say good-bye to Jonathon," she said.

"I've had a word with him. Sykes has been amply paid for his services," he said, not reprimanding her for using the man's first name—as if "Mr. Sykes" were not bad enough!—but stressing the *Sykes*, to remind her he was a servant.

As he spoke, he took her elbow and led her from the house. At least the weather was in their favor. A luminous copper disc in the watery sky suggested it would be a fine day once they got beyond the coastal mist. The breeze from the ocean was not so very chilly. Salverton set a brisk pace, and they arrived at the Curzon before his coachman. They found the lobby virtually empty. He asked for a private parlor and managed to get Samantha hidden away without being seen by anyone but the hotel employees. Then he sent word that his coachman was to wait for him outside.

"This is more like it!" he said when the steaming coffee arrived. The waiter lifted the lids from plates of bacon and eggs. A rack of toast was placed on the table. Pots of marmalade and jam were offered, and they enjoyed a civilized breakfast.

"Does the bruised eye hurt, Edward?" Samantha asked.

"Only my pride. You will recall I was outnumbered last night. I can usually handle myself pretty well in a brawl."

"I noticed you weren't backward about starting the fight."

Salverton was pleased to see no sign of disapproval. He was happy to show her he wasn't just a stiff-rumped worthy, but the sort of gentleman who could pitch himself into a brawl when necessary.

"How will you explain the eye to Lady Louise?" she asked. "Bumped into a door, I believe, is the usual explanation."

"Just so. At least I shan't have to explain this shirt and soiled cravat. I'll change before I call on her. Just a brief visit, and a quick trip to Berkeley Square. I must speak to my secretary, then we'll go on to Tunbridge Wells."

"You got the address of Sir Geoffrey's house from Sykes?"

Salverton's fork stopped halfway to his mouth. "I thought you had it."

"No, I thought you got it when you spoke to him this morning. I know only that the cottage is in Tunbridge Wells."

"Damnation! I'll send my groom back to Sykes's place to get directions."

They were interrupted by a tap at the door. Salverton's face froze. If one of Lady Louise's friends had seen him come in here with Samantha—

Before he had time to think of a story to account for it, the door opened and Jonathon Sykes came striding into the parlor. Jonathon had had no problem with his toilette. He wore a decent blue jacket, a clean shirt and cravat, and a freshly shaved face, and looked, as Salverton was acutely aware, better than himself.

Samantha immediately invited him to join them

for coffee. "You think of everything, Jonathon," she said. "My cousin was just telling me he forgot to get the address of Sir Geoffrey's house in Tunbridge Wells."

Jonathon pulled up a chair and handed her a sheet of paper. "I got the directions from Amy this morning, but that's not the only reason I'm here."

Salverton directed a cold stare at him. "How much? I assume this trip has diverted you from some vastly lucrative enterprise."

"Nay, you've paid me handsomely, melord—unless you want to add a *pourboire* for what I'm about to tell you."

"What is it?" Samantha asked.

"The fellow I warned you about last night. He's still on your tail. I thought it wise to follow you to make sure. He didn't follow you from my place, but he's out front now, keeping an eye on your rig. I figure he went to the stable, knowing you'd collect your rattler and prads before going any farther. He's changed his donkey for a mount, but it's the same lad right enough."

"Who can he be?" Samantha said, looking from Sykes to Salverton.

It was Salverton who answered. "Bow Street, obviously."

Jonathon said, "I could have a dab jostle him. I know a gallows bird would do it for next to nothing."

Salverton began to explain to Samantha. "What Sykes means is that he knows a pickpocket who—"

"I know that, Edward. I'm not a complete flat. You forget my association with Wanda. The man must be from Bow Street, don't you think?" she said, addressing herself to Sykes.

"Of course he is. Who else could he possibly be?" Salverton said. "No need to hire the gallows bird. The officer obviously followed us from London in the hope that we'd lead him to Miss Claridge and Darren. When he sees us return to London, he'll assume we've failed."

"Still, it might be worth checking," Sykes said. "Better safe than sorry."

Salverton assumed Sykes was interested only in further incursions into his purse, and declined the offer.

"It's up to you," Sykes said, "but now that I got a closer look at the fellow, I'm not so sure he's from Bow Street. It's not one of the lads Townsend usually sends to Brighton. I know the regulars to see them. This one's a big, husky brute."

"A good try, Sykes, but I'll stick by my decision," Salverton said. "Thank you. You may leave us now."

Samantha thought Edward had been rather curt and said, "You've been very helpful, Jonathon. Perhaps we'll meet again sometime. If I'm ever in trouble in this part of the country, I shall know whom to call on."

"Your humble servant, Miss Oakleigh."

He bowed, then spoiled the handsome gesture with a broad wink, and left.

"Definitely an original," Samantha said.

Salverton picked up the paper holding the directions to Sir Geoffrey's house in Tunbridge Wells and glanced at it.

"Just this side of Rusthall Common, half a mile north of town," he said. "Sir Geoffrey calls this cottage The Laurels as well. I wonder how many of these Laurels he has scattered about the countryside." He slipped the paper into his pocket. "Shall we go now?"

Samantha picked up her reticule. As Salverton helped her on with her pelisse, a light, flowery scent assailed his nostrils. A pleasant smell, calling to mind wild flowers and meadows—fresh and wholesome. Lady Louise used nothing but French perfume with a heavy, musky scent.

Salverton was relieved to get into his own well-sprung carriage, and especially he was happy to have seen the back of Jonathon Sykes. As they bowled along toward London, he settled in for a friendly chat with Samantha. He decided he should, after all, apologize for barging into her room that morning.

"When I didn't hear a sound," he explained, "I took the notion you had gone tearing off with Sykes again. I'm sorry I caught you *en déshabille*."

She gave him a pert look. "Are you, Edward? I took the notion you were far from unhappy."

He didn't blush, but he looked disconcerted. "I didn't say I didn't enjoy it. Merely I am sorry if I discommoded you."

"You didn't. I wasn't exactly naked, after all."

A small but reckless smile curved his lips. "Not quite," he murmured as a memory of that diaphanous nightgown wafted through his mind.

A spontaneous bubble of laughter erupted from her ripe lips. "I think you ought to get yourself another Esmée, Edward. If you leer at the other ladies the way you leered at me, your fiancée will be disgusted with you."

"*Leer!* I didn't leer! Any man would take a second look at such a— Well, you ain't exactly an antidote, Samantha."

"Why, thank you, Edward. Are you always so effulgent in your compliments to the ladies?"

"What sort of compliments do your other—your beaus offer?"

"Oh, I shan't tell you. It would smack of conceit to say Mr. Abercrombie called me an Incomparable, and Sir Lawrence Chiswick said I was the finest-looking filly that ever walked on two legs."

His lips twitched. "High praise indeed. I see I must step up my flattery if I hope to get anywhere with you."

"I think you mean with Lady Louise," she said demurely.

"Is that what I mean?" he murmured.

"Edward!" She pinned him with a sapient eye. "Are you trying to flirt with me?"

"So it seems. Am I so out of practice that you didn't even recognize it?"

She gave the matter a moment's consideration. "Well, it did sound rather like flirtation, but when I considered the source, I thought perhaps you were being satirical. I'm sure you'll do better when you're with someone other than your cousin."

Samantha felt she had dropped Edward the hint that he was ignoring his body's needs and suggested they play bury all your horses to pass the time.

"I haven't played that since I was in short coats. A white horse counts for two points, if memory serves, and any other color for one."

"A white horse is three points—and the other player must bury all his horses and begin counting over again. Whoever gets a hundred horses first wins."

"What's the prize?" he asked. His glinting smile still held a touch of flirtation.

"We shall play for pennies." He lowered his brow at her. "Or do you not approve of gambling?" she asked, refusing to be the butt of his flirtation. "No matter, we—"

He allowed his gaze to roam over her face, settling on her lips. When he spoke, his voice had again that velvety sound of intimacy. "Let us make it interesting and play for—"

"Edward!"

"Shillings," he said, chewing a grin.

"I couldn't possibly afford it."

"Then I shall just have to think of some forfeit," he said with a rakish grin.

"And to think, Miss Donaldson said I should be perfectly safe with you. She meant it as a compliment, I promise you," she added when he failed to appear pleased with this commendation.

"You are perfectly safe with me, Samantha. No lady ever died of flirtation."

"Unless perhaps of a broken heart when the cruel gentleman was using her only for practice." She raised her hands to her eyes and emitted a few loud, burlesque sniffs. Then she said, "I am only funning, Cousin. I know I am as safe as if I were in church. Safer. Mr. Ambercrombie pinched my bottom on the way out of church last month."

"I wager you didn't let him off with it."

"Certainly not. I turned around and stepped hard on his toe. He knew I did it on purpose. You should have seen his face. He was scarlet with shame. And so he should have been."

When they fell into a short silence, Edward thought over the various things Samantha had said during their adventure. He was appalled at the way she, and probably all the world away from Whitehall, saw him. A man of overweening ambition, a tame man with whom a lady was "perfectly safe" in a carriage, a man who frowned on a bit of innocent gambling. He used to be a wild and reckless buck—and better liked, by and large, than he was now. He had shoals of friends in those days. Now his "friends" were really political cohorts and relatives who approached him only when they wanted a favor.

He sat for some minutes, reviewing his life. Surely he had done the right thing to abandon his licentious ways, to make a career for himself? Lady Louise would never have spared a second glance at the old Lord Salverton. Lord Salty, his friends used to call him. He had soon convinced himself this present mood of dissatisfaction would pass as soon as he found Darren and straightened out the business with Sir Geoffrey and Bow Street. This interval was merely a fling, a little interruption in his usually worthy life.

Samantha was a charming and lovely girl, but a deep-dyed provincial when all was said and done. Not the sort of lady who would make a fitting prime minister's wife, and the prime ministership was his ultimate goal.

Samantha saw she had given him something to think about and didn't disturb him. It was lunchtime when they reached London.

"Would you mind dropping me off at Upper Grosvenor Square?" she said. "Miss Donaldson will be on nettles to know what is happening. I can take a hansom cab back to your place after you've visited Lady Louise."

"Yes, certainly. I should pay my respects to Miss Donaldson. And I shall pick you up after. I don't like to see you taking public conveyances."

Samantha just shook her head. "Trying to make a silk purse out of a sow's ear, Cousin? You'll catch cold at that."

He didn't argue or banter, but just repeated, "I shall call for you, Samantha."

"Perhaps Darren will be home, and our adventure will be over," she said, hoping to please him.

She was surprised when a frown creased his brow. Was it possible Edward was enjoying this escapade? Perhaps he was coming to realize there was more to life than work, and a marriage of convenience to a duke's eldest daughter.

Chapter Ten

In the flat on Upper Grosvenor Square, Miss Donaldson had been on vigil since dawn, waiting in vain for some sign of either Darren or his sister. She was vastly relieved when Salverton's crested carriage came bowling along, and astonished to see Edward himself assist Samantha down. She had hoped he'd lend Samantha his rig, but that he went with her himself was condescension of a high order. Her worries were not over, but they were greatly diminished. She was at the door to welcome them.

"Samantha! And Cousin Edward—so excessively kind of you. Have you any word—"

Lord Salverton bowed formally. "Nice to see you again, Miss Donaldson. We haven't found the miscreants yet, but we are hot on their trail."

"But if they weren't in Brighton—"

"It was a horrid take-in," Samantha said with a touch of asperity, then turned and said familiarly to Edward, "Come on into the saloon, Edward. Let us not stand in the hall like tradesmen."

"Do come in," Miss Donaldson added.

The hallway was dim. In the stronger light of the saloon she noticed that Salverton was wearing evening toilette. It was not in the pristine condition she would have expected, either. And was that the makings of a black eye? She was on thorns to hear their story.

Once settled in the modest saloon, Samantha opened her budget.

"Darren and Wanda didn't go to Sir Geoffrey's cottage in Brighton at all. There was another couple in the cottage. Fortunately Edward knew them, and Mrs. Abercrombie—"

"What on earth was *she* doing there?" Miss Donaldson exclaimed.

"Not the Mrs. Abercrombie from Milford, Auntie. This one was from London, some kin to a bishop. She was extremely sorry she had her footman hit Edward with the poker. Of course, it was only to be expected when Mr. Sykes picked the lock practically in the middle of the night and frightened the poor souls half to death."

"Is that what happened to your eye, Cousin?" Miss Donaldson asked him.

"No," Samantha said for him, "that happened at Mike Skelton's gaming hell last night. I am coming to that."

Miss Donaldson stared as if listening to a performance in Greek. "You mentioned a Mr. Sykes . . ."

"Yes, Jonathon Sykes. He isn't really a groom, but he was kind enough to drive the carriage for us, in case Edward's own coachman should be recognized. Edward was concerned lest his fiancée, Lady Louise St. John, should see him out with me." She turned to Edward. "Do you think Lord Carnford will tell her?"

"Oh, you are engaged, Cousin! I hadn't heard it," Miss Donaldson said. This took precedence even over his being hit with the poker.

"It is not an engagement yet," he said, and added

without undue concern, "God knows whether she'll have me if word of all this gets about."

Mary chose this moment to inform her mistress that luncheon was served.

"I hope you will take lunch with us, Cousin?" Miss Donaldson said. It seemed the least she could do.

"Edward wants to call on Lady Louise, Miss Donaldson," Samantha said. "He was to accompany her to the opera this evening, but it isn't likely he'll be back in time. I shall fill you in on all the details of Brighton while we eat."

"Cousin Edward has to eat as well. There is plenty of food here. You know we were wondering what to do with that ham, Samantha, and I sent Mary out for fresh bread, as ours was gone. Do stay, Cousin. Couldn't you write a note to Lady Louise and explain?"

"I'll be happy to join you," Edward said.

While Mary set the extra places at table, Salverton undertook a proper explanation of their doings over the past twenty-odd hours. Miss Donaldson assumed that Mr. Sykes was a friend of Salverton's who had provided them well-chaperoned sleeping arrangements. The explanations and future plans were so long and complicated that they continued through luncheon, along, of course, with a multitude of questions as to where Darren could be, and whether he would escape without major damage to his reputation.

"At least we needn't fear he'll marry her, Auntie," Samantha said. "Darren would never be fool enough to marry a woman with a daughter nearly as old as herself."

"Married as well as carrying on with Sir Geoffrey! Is there no end to the woman's treachery!"

"Well, there seems some doubt she is married, actually," Samantha said. Miss Donaldson began to fan herself with the corner of her napkin.

"I don't mean to disparage your chaperonage, Miss Donaldson," Salverton said, "but how did you come to let Samantha and Darren caper about the city so freely with this Wanda female?"

Samantha flared up in defense of her chaperon. "Darren is no longer a minor. He can do as he likes. Miss Donaldson tried a dozen times to slow him down, but he would have none of it, and neither would I. If you want to scold someone, scold me. We didn't know Wanda was so—" She tossed up her hands in exasperation. "We were complete greenhorns, Edward. We mistook her fast ways and broad talk for smart London manners. How should we know the difference?"

"You might have called on me sooner," Edward said.

"You cannot lay that in Miss Donaldson's dish, either," Samantha shot back. "She was forever hounding us to call on you, until we were tired of hearing it. I was the one who didn't want to go." She gave Edward a very familiar smile and added, "I thought at the time, you see, that you were a dead bore, Edward."

Edward, whom Miss Donaldson expected to freeze them on the spot with some quelling setdown, said, "I haven't quite the dash of Mr. Sykes, to be sure," and they both laughed.

What was afoot here? Miss Donaldson sensed more than a few shared hours looking for Darren. The way they looked at each other was closer to flirtation than anything else. Cousin Edward flirting? She would as soon expect to see the Pope saying Mass in St. Paul's Cathedral. Mind you, he had been a bit of a lad in his day.

When Edward caught the dame's questioning look, he said, "Your charge has developed a tendre for that scape-gallows Sykes."

"But who is he? Is he not a gentleman?"

Samantha said, "Nearly," at the same moment as Edward gave a snorting, "Hardly!"

"I was joking," Samantha explained, and added an aside to Edward, "Mind your tongue, Lord Salty!"

Miss Donaldson watched and listened in growing confusion. Just exactly what had been the sleeping arrangements at Mr. Sykes's house? When had Samantha begun treating Cousin Edward in this familiar way? And where had she learned he used to be called Lord Salty? That ancient history was buried long before. It seemed this trip had revived a little something of Lord Salty.

When they had finished a cold nuncheon of bread, ham, and cheese, Samantha said, "You should run along and pay your call on Lady Louise, Edward. We want to be back from Tunbridge Wells before dark."

"Perhaps I shall just write Louise a note, as Miss Donaldson suggested."

"Afraid to show your face with that darkened daylight?" she asked pertly.

"I wouldn't want to risk giving the lady a disgust of me," he replied. "I'll write from my own house, and make a fresh toilette while I'm there. I should be back within the hour. We'll reach Tunbridge Wells before dinnertime."

Suddenly Miss Donaldson wasn't so sure Samantha was safe with her cousin.

"Perhaps I should go with you," she said, looking at him with a more critical eye than before.

Salverton hesitated only a moment before replying, "Perhaps that would be best."

It was Samantha who balked at the notion. She was only half done with her job of reforming Edward, if turning him from the path of such rectitude could be called reforming. Miss Donaldson would undo all her work.

"What if Darren comes back while we're gone?" Samantha said. "Someone should be here to keep a rein on him. We shan't be staying overnight, if that is what you're worried about," she added baldly. It was Miss Donaldson who blushed. "We've already stayed at Mr. Sykes's place in Brighton."

"What sort of a place is it? Was there a chaperon?"

Samantha took a deep breath and said, "Of course there was. Mr. Sykes's aunt was there, Miss Mabel Sykes. A very respectable woman. And I can assure you, Edward was a perfect gentleman."

"I'm sure he was," Miss Donaldson said, her fears diminishing. "I would like to be here if Darren comes. How long do you think you'll be gone, Cousin?"

"I'll take my curricle," Edward said at once. "Twenty-five miles both ways. That's four hours. And another hour at most to straighten out Darren. Five hours. The sun sets late in May. We'll be back before dark."

"I suppose it will be all right." It occurred to her that Cousin Edward could go alone. But as she noticed the gleam in his eye when he looked at

Samantha, she wondered if it was a good idea to interfere. What an excellent parti for her! Better than they could have hoped for. He had made a point of saying he was not engaged yet. While Salverton seemed to be relaxing a little on his high morals, he would never think of harming a maiden. That, at least, Lord Salty had never done.

She said, "Why don't you go to Cousin Edward's house with him now, Samantha? It will save his coming back to Upper Grosvenor Square to collect you."

"A good idea," Edward said. "But before we leave, perhaps you would change your bonnet, Samantha."

"Tyrant!" she said, her chin in the air. But Miss Donaldson noticed she hopped off to exchange the bonnet. When she rejoined them, she carried her blue poke bonnet in her hand, and had tamed her tousle of curls. Her bangs had been pulled back and held in place with a pair of combs. She looked more like her old self.

Edward tilted his head to one side and examined her. "You didn't have to go that far," he said. "What have you done to your curls?"

Samantha put the bonnet on with the combs still in place. "There's no pleasing you," she scolded. "Pretty fussy for a man in a dirty shirt and a black eye."

She turned to her chaperon and gave her a hug. "Don't worry, Miss Donny. We'll have the culprit back safe and sound. Edward will lend Darren a thousand pounds to repay Sir Geoffrey. He thinks he can bribe Sir Geoffrey to withdraw the charges. These M.P's know all the shady tricks."

At this left-handed compliment, Lord Salverton

smiled blandly and made his adieus to Miss Donaldson, who sat on in the saloon alone for the next hour, wondering if she had done the right thing to let Samantha go with him. It was a calculated risk, but the prize was so grand that she didn't see how she could in good conscience have denied Samantha her chance at such a good title and fortune.

Salverton's carriage soon drew up in front of the familiar mansion on Berkeley Square. Lord Salverton's butler stared with disbelief at his master's discolored eye and wilting shirt points. His gimlet eye slewed to Miss Oakleigh, whom he suspected to be the cause of this wanton disarray.

"Shall I call your valet, your lordship?" Luten inquired.

"Later. For the present, you may call Plimpton for me."

"Yes, sir."

"Who's Plimpton?" Samantha asked as they went to his study.

"My secretary."

"I hope he is less daunting than your butler. I don't know how you can stand having that Friday-faced creature scowling at you every time you enter your own house. It would be enough to give me the megrims."

"You never get the megrims. You told me so yourself. Luten is an excellent butler."

He held the door and Samantha went into the study, to see a handsome young fellow sitting at Lord Salverton's desk, apparently rifling his drawers.

"Miss Oakleigh, allow me to present my secretary, Mr. Plimpton," Edward said.

Plimpton leapt to his feet. A pair of twinkling blue eyes opened wider upon first viewing Miss Oakleigh. "Oh, I say! How do you do, ma'am." In his astonishment, he forgot to bow.

"Anything important in the mail?" Salverton asked.

"Oodles of notes from Whitehall. Er, what happened to you, Salverton? Bumped into a door?"

"Just so. May I know why you've usurped my office during my absence?"

"I was just looking for that letter from the chancellor. It was to be answered by today. I have your notes. I was going to write it up and send it off."

Salverton turned to Samantha. "My secretary is also excellent. I am hardly required here at all." He turned back to Plimpton. "I shall need a couple of hundred pounds, Peter. I'll be leaving almost immediately. Would you please write a note to Lady Louise telling her I shan't be able to accompany her to the opera, but shall call later if I'm back in time."

"You'll sign it yourself?"

"Yes, leave it on my desk."

"What excuse shall I give her?"

"The *reason* is an urgent family matter that requires my attention."

"I'm sorry to delay you, Salverton, but there's also that report that requires your immediate attention."

"Quite. Come upstairs with me while I make a toilette. Bring your notebook. We'll discuss it there."

Plimpton darted into the next room and returned with a stack of papers and a notebook.

"I shan't be a moment, Samantha," Salverton

said. "Help yourself to a glass of wine. If you require anything else, call Luten. He won't bite you—if he knows what is good for him. I have no doubt you'd bite back."

On that speech, Salverton strode from the room. Plimpton cast one questioning glance on Miss Oakleigh before darting off after his employer. He was familiar enough with Salverton to know something unusual was afoot. Miss Oakleigh was very different from the cousins who usually came begging at the door, and Salverton was treating her differently, too. Very odd, that. Salverton didn't usually have any use for those pert girls. Mind you, she was dashed pretty.

Chapter Eleven

While Salverton's fresh toilette was proceeding above stairs, his secretary discussed the correspondence with him and took notes on how various matters were to be handled. The last item was for Plimpton to discover Sir Geoffrey Bayne's address and call on him personally to repay the purloined thousand pounds.

"I'll write you a check on my bank. Give him cash, but get a receipt promising he'll drop the charge. I want the only record of this arrangement in my own pocket. If he turns rusty, you can hint at some future perk. I'll see what I can arrange."

The gentlemen then returned to the study, where Samantha had made herself at home. She was writing a note to her friend at Milford.

"I wanted to show off your crested stationery," she explained artlessly.

"Be sure to have me frank it before you send it off," Salverton said, chewing back a smile. "Receiving it without expense is more likely to impress your friend than the crest."

"I wanted to ask you, but was afraid you'd cut up stiff," she said.

"You will be giving Plimpton a strange notion of my character, Cousin."

"A regular tartar," Plimpton said, smiling in a bold way that belied the statement.

Salverton called for his curricle while Plimpton got cash from the safe.

When this was done, Salverton said, "Write the note to Lady Louise first, Plimpton. I want to sign it before I leave. You can sign for me on the other matters." Then he turned to his guest. "Samantha, a glass of wine while we wait?"

The door knocker sounded as Plimpton was leaving. Salverton gave a tsk of annoyance and said to his secretary, "Tell Luten I'm not in—unless it's the P.M."

Samantha felt a little thrill to consider that she might be about to meet this eminent worthy. They both listened as Luten spoke to the caller. It was Plimpton who appeared first at the study door. His face wore a harassed expression.

"It's Lady Louise!" he said in a strangled whisper. "Luten's let her in."

"Damn the man!" Salverton growled.

Samantha knew she was the cause of his discomfiture. Lady Louise would dislike that her fiancé (nearly) was involving himself in such low doings for a female cousin who was not precisely an antidote. Naturally the lady would be jealous if she had any affection at all for Edward. Samantha felt instinctively that if she could allay the lady's jealousy, all would be well. She thought Edward was making a mistake to marry the duke's daughter, but he must see the light for himself. She would not be the cause of his losing out on her, if that was what he truly wanted. She waited eagerly to see this lady, who had recently been featuring largely in her thoughts.

The lady who came striding into the study was obviously from the very top of the tallest tree in the country. She was elegantly outfitted in a blue walking suit and dashing high poke bonnet. Pride and arrogance deprived a handsome face of its beauty. The physical requirements of an Incomparable were all there—glossy black hair, fine white skin, dark and lustrous eyes, and a well-shaped nose. What was lacking was that spark of amiability. The lips were held in a thin line. The eyes glittered in vexation.

"Salverton, why did you not call this morning?" she demanded in a strident tone. Then she looked around and spotted Samantha sitting at his desk, holding his pen, looking as if she owned the place, and her lips grew thinner.

Salverton said, "Louise, allow me to introduce my cousin, Miss—"

Samantha leapt from the chair as if it had grown spikes. "I'm Mrs. Oakleigh," she said, advancing to Lady Louise and curtsying low. "And you, I take it, are Lady Louise. Such an honor to meet you. Lord Salverton has spoken of you, milady."

Samantha didn't risk a glance at Edward, but she could sense his astonishment.

"Mrs. Oakleigh, you say?" Lady Louise said. Her annoyance lessened a degree.

"Married to Lord Salverton's cousin, Darren Oakleigh," Samantha invented. "When my Darren fell into a hobble, I didn't know where to turn, so I asked Lord Salverton to lend a hand. He is always so helpful in family matters. I am extremely sorry it caused him to miss your tea party. He was most distressed."

Lady Louise was sufficiently mollified to inquire the nature of Mr. Oakleigh's hobble.

With one glare at Samantha, Salverton spoke up swiftly to forestall talk of lightskirts and stolen money. "He's disappeared," he said. "I am trying to find him. I'm afraid, Louise, that I may not be able to attend the opera this evening. I was just about to—"

"Salverton was just going to call on you," Samantha said, feeling this would be more flattering than to have his secretary write a letter.

"Your first trip to London, Mrs. Oakleigh?" Lady Louise inquired with a careful examination of the lady's toilette.

"Indeed, yes, milady, and I hope it may be our last, for I fear London is too big and wicked for Darren and me. I wager he has been caught up in some card game, like a regular flat."

"If you are fortunate, it may be no more than that. You ought to check out the hospitals, Salverton, and the morgue. The city is full of cutthroat bandits." On this speech, Job's Comforter turned toward the door. "If you find him in time, do come to the opera this evening, Salverton. I shan't give anyone else your seat. We were to attend with Mama and Papa, so I shan't be alone. Good day, Mrs. Oakleigh."

"Thank you, ma'am," Samantha said in a chastened voice.

Salverton accompanied Lady Louise to the front door. "Pity," the lady said to him. "Could you not send Plimpton to look for this Darren person?"

"A family matter," Salverton murmured vaguely. "I felt I ought to lend a hand."

"You're too generous by half, Salverton. You can't

forsake your job at Whitehall for every provincial cousin who falls into a hobble. They're debating the budget in the House today. You ought to be there. Why don't people like that stay in the country, where they belong?"

"It is the Oakleighs' wedding trip," he said, and was astonished at the celerity with which this lie occurred to him.

"Are they prominent in their home riding?"

"Very influential," he said, to be rid of her without further squabbling.

"The fellow is probably drunk in some ditch. Find him quickly, for you must attend my ball tomorrow evening. Papa expects it." Her meaningful look suggested why this should be so.

She cast a commanding eye on Luten, who flew to hold the door for her. She swept out. A footman in royal blue with gold lace held the door of an extremely elegant crested carriage that stood at the curb. The lady entered and was carried off without a backward glance.

Salverton said, "No more callers," to Luten, and returned to the study to find Samantha and Plimpton enjoying a fit of giggles.

"You should be on the stage, Miss Oakleigh," Plimpton said. "Upon my word, you should."

"Or in Bridewell," Salverton added curtly.

"Surely it is not an indictable offense to tell a little social lie," Samantha retorted, "even to a duke's eldest daughter."

"You can forget the letter to Lady Louise, Plimpton," Salverton said, and turned a wrathful eye on his cousin. "May I know the reason for that unnecessary performance? It will be awkward, if you meet Lady Louise again in the future, to explain how your husband has suddenly become your brother."

"I was afraid she'd beat the pair of us if she learned the truth. You must be sure not to bring her to Milford after the wedding. You're a brave man, Edward, to shackle yourself to that tartar. Of course she is very handsome—and well dowered, I should think?"

"Thirty thousand," Plimpton said.

"That much!" Samantha exclaimed. "Well then, you wouldn't want to risk alienating her by helping me. Carnford may run to her with his story. Only marriage could restore me to respectability, and you to your usual unassailable position of rectitude. From the way she orders you about, I assume the engagement is all but settled?"

"I have some reason to believe she would accept an offer," he said, but his mind was dwelling on that "unassailable position of rectitude." He had thought Samantha realized by now that he was human.

"Then I wish you well," she said in a voice that implied he would need all the luck he could find.

They went out to the waiting curricle, drawn by a set of blood grays.

"It must be lovely to have so many carriages and horses," Samantha said as he handed her up.

Before Salverton could join her, a coachman came up to them, shouting. "Here, milord! Wait a moment!"

"Good Lord!" Salverton moaned. "It's Sykes! What the devil can he want?"

Sykes was panting as he approached the curricle. "Glad I caught you in time!"

"Well, what is it?" Salverton demanded.

"It's that fellow who was following us last night. He ain't a Bow Street runner. I checked him out with my pals. When I learned that, I set out after you. He's followed you from Brighton. I spotted his rig around the corner on Bruton Street. He's waiting to follow you again."

"I didn't notice anyone following us," Salverton said, frowning.

"You wasn't looking. He's there right enough. What does the likes of him want with you and Miss Oakleigh? I thought I'd best let you know."

"Thank you, Sykes," Salverton said, reaching into his pocket for the necessary *pourboire.*

Sykes pocketed the money and said jauntily, "Where are we off to, then? Tunbridge Wells, is it?"

"Miss Oakleigh and I are going to Tunbridge Wells," Salverton said. "I suggest you return to Brighton."

"My nag's winded from following you. When I saw the villain who's been dogging your heels stop at Bruton Street, I rode over to Newman's stable and hired a rig. I was just about to knock on your door, when the duchess came out. Or thinks she's a duchess anyhow, with her nose in the air."

"A duchess's eldest daughter, actually," Samantha told him. Then she spoke to Salverton. "About that man following us, Edward. We can't just ignore him. He may mean to do Darren a mischief."

"He's a rough customer," Sykes said. "I noticed he carried a pistol. He stopped to wet his whistle at Grinstead. I followed him into the tavern. That's when I seen it. You don't want to put the lady in jeopardy, melord. It ain't seemly. You'd best let me come along with you. We'll want a closed carriage. I took the liberty of hiring an unmarked one at

Newman's, knowing you wasn't anxious to have your crest seen before at Brighton."

"A complete hand," Samantha said to Edward. "I do think he's right, Cousin. This curricle offers poor security if the man decides to use that pistol."

"Couldn't you discover who he is?" Salverton asked Sykes.

"I meant to break it to you gentle," he said, aiming his words at Samantha. "I fear it's bad news. Me pals tell me he calls hisself Mortimer Fletcher, a London rogue. Fletch, for everyday use. He's just out of Newgate, where he did ten years. He would have been Jack Ketch's breakfast but for the lack of a witness to the man he kilt."

"Good gracious!" Samantha exclaimed, and grew pale. "What can he want with us?"

"As you two have done nothing, I h'assume he's following you to find Darren. Or Wanda—or both of 'em. P'raps Sir Geoffrey hired him. You'll want another pair of fists when you do find them. I'll try to lose Fletcher along the way. I know a few spots where we might manage it."

"Very well," Salverton said. "Where is this unmarked hired carriage, Sykes?"

"Just around the corner. I'll bring it forward while you send this rig back to the stable. Handsome prads, melord. Sixteen miles an hour, I wager."

"Yes, pity we won't be using them," Salverton said.

His instinct was to tell Sykes to go to the devil, and continue on in the open carriage with Samantha. He had been looking forward to the trip with considerable pleasure, but he couldn't put her life in jeopardy on a mere whim. He sensed, too, that

Sykes—damn his eyes—would be a good man in a brawl.

It was some small consolation that Sykes was handling the ribbons of the carriage. At least he wouldn't be inside with them for the entire trip. He was also an unexceptionable fiddler who was intimately acquainted with all the roads of England, to hear him speak, at least. The horses looked like goers as well. Salverton wondered what outrageous sum he'd have to pay Sykes for having hired them.

It occurred to him that Sykes might have invented this villain following them, until he peered out the rear window and saw the unmarked sporting carriage. The bays drawing it looked like excellent horses. It was impossible to get a good look at the driver. He had his hat pulled low over his eyes, but he was a big brute, with shoulders as broad as the Parthenon.

With all this in his dish and missing the opera besides, it quite amazed Salverton that he could still feel relatively cheerful. He kept a sharp eye on the carriage behind them. The driver was crafty enough to allow a few carriages between his rig and his quarry's, but he was always there, dogging their steps. He cast a shadow over what would otherwise have been a thoroughly enjoyable outing.

"Don't worry so, Edward," Samantha said when he checked the rear window half a dozen times. "Mr. Sykes will lose him. He is an excellent fiddler."

This, unaccountably, only worsened her cousin's mood.

Chapter Twelve

The top finger of the signpost said TONBRIDGE. The finger below it said TUNBRIDGE WELLS, SIX MILES. The drive through the fertile Weald south of the North Downs had been pleasant, but a few side excursions and ruses had not succeeded in shaking Fletcher from their tail.

"Has Sykes forgotten he was going to escape from Fletcher?" Edward said.

"He hasn't forgotten. I'm sure he has some plan," Samantha replied calmly.

They soon entered Tonbridge, an ancient, timbered market town. Salverton assumed Sykes would drive through the village and continue southward. Instead, the carriage was driven to a recreational area on the banks of the Medway. Before there was time to inquire, Sykes was at the window.

"Time to lose Fletch if we're ever going to," he said. "He likes his ale, does Fletch. He gargled down three at Grinstead while I had one. I figured if we could convince him we was making a longish stop, he'd not be able to resist the temptation to wet his whistle. If you and Miss Oakleigh care to alight and go for a stroll, melord, I'll handle Fletch."

"What do you plan to do?" Salverton asked.

"Go to the Chequers Inn for a bite. He'll figure

the carriage can't leave without me, and take the chance to have a wet. I'll linger a spell at the inn, p'raps fool him entirely by hiring a room and going up to it, while you drive the rig out of sight. When he comes back here to check out the rig, I'll slip out of the inn and meet you on a back road. Not the main road to Tunbridge Wells, mind. That's where Fletch will be looking for you when he sees the carriage is gone. There's another small road that heads south as well. It don't go directly to Tunbridge Wells, but a mile beyond the city there's a turnoff. Take it and backtrack to Tunbridge Wells."

"That's ingenious, Mr. Sykes!" Samantha exclaimed.

Salverton couldn't think of a better plan, but he contained his enthusiasm. "Where do I find this smaller road?"

"Turn around and go back the way we came. Just before you come to that half-timbered farmhouse on your left, you'll see an unmetaled road. It looks a mite rough. It don't get better, but it don't get worse, either. And what do we care, eh? The rattler and prads are hired."

"Spoken like a scoundrel!" Salverton muttered, but he agreed to the plan.

Salverton and Samantha alit. He put his hand on her elbow and they began a walk along the banks of the Medway, stopping to watch some children floating toy boats. From the corners of their eyes they saw Sykes drive the rig into the parking area and leave on foot for the main street. After a moment Fletch drove by. When he spotted the carriage, he also drew into the parking area at the far end, looking back over his shoulder to see where his quarry were going.

"Buy us an ice," Samantha suggested. "He'll think you can't go to the tavern because of me."

"You're becoming as bossy as Lady Louise," Salverton said.

She gave him a saucy look. "Is she bossy, Edward?"

"Outspoken, I should have said," he replied.

He bought two ices. As he handed one to Samantha, he saw Fletch leave his carriage and follow Sykes. As Fletch's broad back disappeared around the corner, Salverton headed to the man's carriage.

"What are you doing?" Samantha asked. "Salverton! Are you going to disable his carriage? How clever! You're becoming nearly as sneaky as Mr. Sykes."

Salverton had intended no more than searching the carriage to try to discover what Fletcher's business might be, but when he heard Samantha's idea, he decided to act on it. He and Samantha strolled about the parking area, seemingly examining the various equipages and nags. When the guard lost interest in them, Edward tossed his ice aside, removed a clasp knife from his pocket, and began cutting the leather straps of the reins. Samantha kept the team quiet by stroking them and speaking in the dulcet tones of a horse lover. One of the horses discovered her ice, and with one flick of his big tongue removed the ice from the cone. Salverton continued working until he had severed every strap. When he had finished, he made a quick examination of the rig, but found nothing to identify the driver.

He said, "Let's go now, before Fletch comes back."

"That horse ate my ice, Edward!"

"A small price to pay."

"I was quite enjoying it. Couldn't I have another? It's very hot and dry."

"Oh, very well." He would have enjoyed another ice himself, but he had to drive.

He bought her the ice and they returned to their carriage. A few heads turned to see a gentleman in such an elegant blue jacket driving his own rig, but then, the Corinthians were up to anything. It was a common sight to see one of them take the reins of the mail coach.

He turned the carriage around and retraced the road to the half-timbered house on the corner. The unpaved road was there where Sykes had said, half hidden by a dense stand of thorn bushes. It looked extremely rough, with holes as big as boilers. They drove through a virtual tree tunnel. Tree branches intruded into the carriage's path, brushing at Salverton's face as they advanced, but the road was passable.

Six miles seemed an eternity, being jostled up and down and eating dust. After half an hour Salverton stopped to check the horses. Samantha got out and joined him. She had removed her bonnet in the carriage and didn't bother to replace it. Her hair had sprung loose from its combs to wanton about her cheeks.

"It's very bumpy inside," she said. "I had to close the windows because of the dust. I'm stifling with the heat."

"Would you like to trade places?" he asked irritably, brushing dust and dead leaves from his shoulders. He drew out his handkerchief and wiped the perspiration from his brow.

Samantha drew her bottom lip between her teeth. "That was thoughtless of me. And when you were kind enough to buy me a second ice, too. Gracious, you look a mess! Here, let me help. You're only making it worse."

She took the handkerchief and began wiping at his face, where the perspiration and dust had combined to leave rivulets of mud on his forehead.

"Bend down," she ordered like a mother speaking to a child.

"I can't. I have a crick in my back from bending under that low ceiling of trees."

"Sit down on that rock, then," she suggested. "I can hardly reach you."

He took her hand and led her to a rock that stood by the edge of an apple orchard. He sat down with a weary sigh and lifted his face to the sun. A stray breeze blew over him, carrying the scent of newly mown hay and clover. The brilliant azure sky above was unmarred by a single puff of cloud. A noisy jay went squalling from one of the apple trees.

Samantha began to wipe away the dirt. She noticed the fine lines on Edward's forehead, and felt a twinge of sympathy for him. Once the bird left, it was almost unnaturally quiet. The only sound was the whisper of the breeze through the treetops and the soft chewing of the team that had taken advantage of the rest to chomp at the grassy verge.

"This really needs water. A pity there isn't a stream. We could water the horses while we're here," she said.

When Salverton didn't reply, she lowered her gaze to his eyes. He was staring at her in a dazed sort of way.

He felt that same softening inside that he had felt in the carriage the night before, when Samantha was stroking his brow. Only this time he could see her as she leaned above him, with her full breasts only inches from him. Sunlight glinted on her blond curls, turning them to a golden cloud, backed by that azure sky. She seemed unreal, like one of those mischievous angels in a Renaissance painting. Her eyes, gazing into his, were fanned by long lashes. As he gazed, her ripe lips trembled open to say something.

For the first time in many a long year, Edward lost control of himself. He pulled her down onto his knee and wrapped both his arms close around her. As her soft breasts melted against his chest, his lips found hers and firmed in a hot embrace that sent his blood flaming like wildfire through his veins and throbbing in his throat. It was a momentary madness, completely out of character, yet irresistible. Strangely, Samantha didn't resist, either. She not only let him kiss her, she kissed him back. His heart pumped harder when he felt her arms go around his neck, tentatively at first, then squeezing gently. Her fingers moved disturbingly in the hair at the nape of his neck, sending dangerous quivers up his spine.

The last two days had seemed unreal to Edward, like some special magical period apart from reality, and as the kiss lingered, he knew that the past hours had been leading ineluctably to this moment. He had wanted to kiss those cherry lips from the moment Samantha had come into his study with those horrid coquelicot ribbons on her bonnet. Or perhaps it was when she had removed her pelisse and he realized that she had grown into a charmer that he had first felt this urge. Her provincial manners and outspokenness should have disgusted him. In theory, they did. But in fact, they excited him. They made her seem less a lady, and more a woman.

As the moment's madness subsided, Samantha withdrew from his arms and stood up. She felt shaken at what had just happened. She had let him kiss her out of curiosity, to see if Salverton was as cold-blooded as he pretended—and perhaps, she admitted, because she just wanted him to kiss her. She hadn't realized a simple kiss could so swiftly accelerate to passion. She saw at once that Edward was as shaken as she was herself. He didn't know what to say. His scarlet past was too far behind him to make him comfortable during this little contretemps.

She playfully lifted a finger and said, smiling, "Now, Cousin, you promised Miss Donny you would behave. We shall forget this happened, if you please, and continue on our way. There, I'm being bossy again." She hoped he hadn't noticed that she was breathless.

Salverton rose. "Samantha—I'm sorry. That was unforgivable. A moment's madness. You were so close, and—"

She gave him a saucy look. "And you are still young enough to succumb to temptation. Well, that is something, anyway."

She walked calmly to the carriage and let herself in. Salverton stood looking after her. He had never seen a lady move so gracefully, with a lithe, swaying motion in her hips. Her waist was ridiculously small. He wanted to go after her and kiss her again. Lord, he had thought he was over that schoolboy fever for women. What must she think of him? He must show her by his behavior during the rest of this escapade that he was completely trustworthy. But there lingered at the back of his mind the fact that she hadn't tried to stop him.

While he drove the carriage along the rutted path, his mind wandered to Lady Louise. He had been courting her for six months, and never felt the least urge to misbehave so shamelessly as he had with Samantha. He hadn't felt that way about any of the pretty girls who were regularly thrown at his head. They had all seemed alike. He must marry, and since the girls were all alike, why not choose the best-born and best-dowered of them? Except that he no longer wanted to marry Lady Louise.

How could he, when he felt like this about Samantha Oakleigh? Of course it wasn't love, he told himself severely. It was merely one of those powerful fascinations that would soon run itself to a standstill, and it was a great pity that it should have occurred just then, when he was on the verge of success with Louise.

Samantha argued with herself, too, as she was jostled along the rutted path. She really shouldn't have let Edward kiss her like that. It was for the lady to impose boundaries. If she had behaved more like a lady, he would have treated her like one. He obviously thought her no better than she should be. He would never lose control like that with Lady Louise. He respected her too much. She would behave with a good deal more propriety from now on. But she felt that if he wanted to kiss her again, she would be hard pressed to deny him. It had been a surprisingly warm kiss.

He hadn't seemed like Lord Salverton at all when he attacked her. He had seemed more like Lord Salty. That wilder side of Edward hadn't died; it was still there, dormant, waiting to burst out when his guard was down, and she liked him better for it. She was relieved when the end of the road was finally in sight. The tree tunnel thinned, and at its end stood Jonathon Sykes, his legs apart, arms akimbo. He came forward, wearing his usual jaunty grin.

"I see you made it, melord."

"Did you manage to lose Fletcher?" Salverton asked.

"He's loitering about town. I booked myself a room for the night, paid for it—I'll add it to your bill. I managed to slip out the back door of the inn. We'd best head straight to Tunbridge Wells, if you'll just hop down and let a fiddler take hold of the reins, melord."

Salverton was already in a bad mood. He didn't think it was by chance that Sykes cast these aspersions on his driving. A "fiddler" indeed! Salverton was well known for his skill in handling the ribbons. And of course Samantha was listening to every word.

"Well done, Mr. Sykes!" she called from the lowered window. Sykes, the demmed jackanapes, bowed low.

Salverton climbed down and let himself into the carriage. If he waited for Sykes to open the door, no doubt another pound would be added to his bill.

The atmosphere in the carriage was strained. Each was determined to forget what had happened in the tree tunnel, and behave with the utmost propriety.

"How is the crick in your back, Cousin?" Samantha asked when they had driven a few hundred yards without speaking.

"Improving. If I just lay my head back against the squabs, it will pass."

He did this, and closed his eyes into the bargain, which would have made conversation difficult if there had been any. As neither of them could think of anything to say, there was no talk until they were nearly at Tunbridge Wells.

"We're nearly there," Samantha said then.

Salverton opened his eyes and looked out the window at picturesque hills and moorland. "Pretty," he said. "My aunt used to come here for the chalybeate waters."

"What are chalybeate waters? Are they like the horrid sulphur water at Bath?"

"Equally horrid, but flavored with iron instead of sulphur. You can try a glass at the Pump Room, if you like."

"I would rather have a nice cup of tea."

"So would I. As soon as we find Darren, we'll have tea, then head straight back to London."

"That will be nice," she said primly.

After this stilted exchange, they both turned to look out the window, where a lively scene greeted them. As they drew into the town, carriages of all sorts were plentiful, as were holidayers. The company was not composed entirely of valetudinarians come to take the waters. There were a few families and a liberal sprinkling of lightskirts come to prey on the elderly gentlemen.

"Jonathon knows where Sir Geoffrey's house is," Samantha said.

"Of course he does. He knows everything."

Samantha saw that her companion was still in one of his moods, and said no more. If it weren't so ridiculous, she would think Edward was jealous of Mr. Sykes.

Chapter Thirteen

Sykes drew the carriage to a stop at the edge of town and climbed down to speak to melord and Miss Oakleigh.

"You have the directions to The Laurels?" Salverton said, ready with the directions himself in the unlikely case that Sykes was capable of forgetting anything.

"Just this side of Rusthall Common, half a mile north."

"Let us proceed there at once."

"I was thinking," Sykes said, adopting a pensive attitude that displayed his handsome profile to Miss Oakleigh. "A dasher like Wanda wouldn't be sitting indoors on her thumbs on a fine day like this. She'd have her young man take her on the strut."

"Of course! Wanda is a regular road hog. Where do you think they would be, Mr. Sykes?" Samantha asked eagerly, taking the man's word for gospel.

"Only one place to go in Tunbridge Wells. The Pantiles."

"Where is that?"

He erupted into a burst of Jovian laughter. "Bless me, you don't know nuthin'. It's what they call the Parade, a promenade in the heart of town.

Folks go on the strut to see and be seen, visit the shops to pick up knickknacks, have a bite to eat or a drink. All the crack. I'll show you."

Salverton directed a cold, commanding stare at his driver. The wretch was right, as usual, but that didn't mean he must stick to them like a burr.

"Stable the rig close by. Miss Oakleigh and I will make a quick tour of the Parade. Wait for us outside the Pump Room. We'll meet you there, with or without Mr. Oakleigh."

"You don't figure you might want an extra pair of fists, in case the lad cuts up stiff?"

"I can handle Mr. Oakleigh, Sykes." Salverton's tone suggested he could also handle Sykes, and would enjoy doing so.

"Just as you say, melord. I'll see you at the Pump Room when you get there. Good luck!" He touched his hat, smiled in Samantha's direction, and returned to the carriage, stopping at the near end of the Pantiles to let his passengers dismount.

There was an awkward moment while Samantha wondered whether she should take Edward's arm, and he wondered whether he should offer it. Neither felt comfortable making the first move, so they began walking along side by side without touching. They walked down the colonnaded side, peering at the pedestrians and into shops for a sight of Wanda and Darren. As Salverton had never seen Wanda and hadn't seen Darren for five years, he hardly knew whom they were looking for.

Whenever he spotted a dark-haired lightskirt, he would point her out and ask, "Would that be her?"

"No, she's taller and better-looking."

"How about this one?" he asked a moment later, when a flashing-eyed bit of muslin leered at him.

"Gracious, Edward! She's not so vulgar! We would have known enough to stay away from a creature like that. Wanda looks ladylike—in comparison to that vulgar jade, I mean."

"I wonder if Darren would be fool enough to be prancing about in public when Bow Street is looking for him."

"He doesn't know they're looking for him. I'm sure he thinks the money belonged to Wanda, and *she* has the nerve for anything. Very likely Mr. Sykes is right, and we'll find them in a shop, spending Sir Geoffrey's blunt."

At one end of the Pantiles stood the seventeenth-century church of King Charles the Martyr. As they passed in front of it to the other side of the promenade, a youngster rolling a hoop nearly capsized Samantha. Edward instinctively reached to steady her. When they continued their walk down the other side, he continued holding her arm. Samantha gave him an uncertain glance, wondering if she should detach herself from him.

"Let me hold your arm," he said. "It might discourage the hussy in the red curls who's been following us."

Samantha looked behind, and saw there was indeed a saucy redhead with her eye on Edward. Samantha felt a jolt of annoyance out of all proportion to the incident. It should have been amusing, but she was not amused. She gave the woman a cutting stare and took a closer hold of Salverton's arm. They continued their walk, always keeping a sharp eye out for their quarry. The lime trees provided shade on their side of the promenade, but were an impediment to keeping an eye on the other side of the road.

They went into various trinket shops. Samantha was lured into buying a pin box of wood mosaic Tunbridgeware for Miss Donaldson. Salverton looked about for some less common little gift he might buy for Samantha, but found nothing to please him. At that end of the Parade stood the Pump Room, with Jonathon Sykes standing guard.

"They're not here," Sykes announced. "I've had a look in the Pump Room as well."

"We'll go on to The Laurels," Salverton said.

"That's a bit of a problem, melord."

Salverton lifted an imperious eyebrow. "Trouble with the carriage? The horses?"

"Neither one. The trouble is, Fletch has turned up. I ducked inside when I saw him, but he'd have spotted the pair of you and will be keeping an eye on you from some dark corner."

"How could he be here so soon?"

"He came on horseback. Something must have happened to his rig. I thought of putting it out of commission, but knew he'd only hire a nag, and there'd be no outrunning him on the road."

Salverton looked at Samantha and noticed her lips were moving unsteadily. He didn't mention having cut the reins.

Sykes continued. "He's ridden on to Tunbridge Wells and got here not five minutes behind us. Pity. We'll have to take evasive action. We don't want to lead him to Darren and Wanda."

"I don't know what he can want with Darren," Samantha said, furrowing her brow. "It must be Wanda he's after."

"P'raps she was in on the robbery he was put in jail for, and he's after her to recover the loot," Sykes suggested. "Wouldn't surprise me much."

"I don't care if he does find her," Samantha said. "Let us go on to The Laurels, Mr. Sykes."

"Fletch is a rough customer. If Wanda was his bit of skirt, he'd not let your brother off unharmed. He's killed before, though they couldn't prove it."

"Oh, dear! In that case, I daresay we must take evasive action. What do you suggest, Mr. Sykes?"

"Food," he said firmly. "You're beginning to look peaky, Samantha. The rosebuds are fading from your dainty cheeks. You must feed yourself. It will soon be coming on dark. Easier to lose Fletch under cover of darkness."

Samantha was ravenous. An ice was no luncheon for a busy girl. It had been hours since they had eaten, and might be hours before another opportunity arose. She gave Sykes a grateful smile.

"Tea would be nice," she said to Salverton.

"And don't you worry about Fletcher, my dear," Sykes said. "I'll lure him off for you. You just take this young lady to a tearoom and feed her, melord. The Tunbridge Tearoom does a dandy tea. Lord Egremont always took his lady there when they was on the strut here in town. You won't be rubbing elbows with the muslin company there. Shocking how bold the lasses are becoming. One of them all but shanghaied me into a doorway. I had to put up quite a fight."

"They've been giving Salverton the eye as well!" Samantha said indignantly.

"They'll throw their bonnets at anyone," Sykes scowled. Salverton bridled up like an angry mare. "Not that I mean to deeneegrate your phiz, melord. My meaning was that even you being stiff as starch and with a charmer like Miss Oakleigh hanging on your lucky arm isn't enough to stop them. They'd proposition an archbishop—and be taken up on the offer, too, to judge by what I know of the clergy."

Salverton felt obliged to defend the clergy. "Your ecclesiastical acquaintances must be quite different from mine," he said.

"I avoid the lot of them as much as I can. Freeloaders! What more do they know of the almighty than you and me?"

"How will you lose Fletcher?" Samantha asked, to avert a religious argument, for she saw that Salverton was ready to take issue with Sykes's views.

Sykes patted the side of his nose with one finger and assumed a wise expression. "H'expediency," he said. "There's the ticket. I'll lose him, never fear, and go to the Tunbridge Tearoom to meet you after the sun's set. You eat up now, miss. Don't rush yourself. Tell Meggie that Sykes sent you. She'll do you up a proper tea."

He darted off before Salverton could exert his authority by naming a different tearoom.

"I don't know which of them is more capable, Fletch or Mr. Sykes," Samantha said, adding to Salverton's ill humor. "It begins to seem that Mr. Sykes has met his match. Fancy Fletcher getting here so soon after you disabled his carriage."

"You're the one who suggested it! How was I supposed to know he'd hire a horse?" Of course he should have known. Sykes would have known.

"You need your tea, Edward. You're becoming quite testy. I wasn't accusing you of foolishness."

They looked around and found the tearoom Sykes had ordered them to. It was more than respectable. The tables wore linen nappery and a vase of flowers. The service was good, and the tea and sandwiches both plentiful and tasty.

Salverton's mood softened in this civilized atmosphere, away from Sykes.

"These delays make it unlikely you'll be able to join Lady Louise at the opera," Samantha said in an apologetic tone.

"That's one advantage, at any rate," Salverton replied. It struck him that he had never liked the opera. One had to go, from time to time, to please the ladies, but really it was a dead bore. The current vogue for Italian tenors especially displeased him.

"Don't you like it?" she asked, surprised.

"No, I don't."

"Then why do you go?"

"It is expected of one," he said stiffly.

Samantha just shook her head. "You spend your days doing what is expected of you, Edward. Surely you could have your evenings to yourself. Even a peasant has that much freedom."

He sipped his tea, trying to remember the last time he had had an evening to do what he wanted to do. Not since taking up with Lady Louise. If he wasn't working nights at the House, he was accompanying Louise to some musical soirée, or the opera, or a ball or rout, usually of her choosing. Did he really want to spend the rest of his life doing such things? Surely there was more to life than that.

"One does what one must," he said vaguely.

"*One!* You're not 'one.' You're you! My goodness, when are you ever going to enjoy yourself if you don't do it now? I noticed this afternoon that you have a few gray hairs, and some little wrinkles on your forehead. You're no longer a boy."

"Don't talk like that!" he said gruffly. "I'm only in my thirties. You make me sound like Methuselah."

"Oh, no. He had nearly a millennium to live. You have only forty odd years left—if you're lucky. Papa died at fifty-nine. He was a worrier and worker like you. Perhaps that's why I feel comfortable with you, despite your—strict ways."

"I'm glad you feel comfortable with me," he said, and decided to venture into forbidden territory. "I was afraid, after this afternoon, you might feel otherwise."

"I did, for a few hours, but it's over now. It's foolish to let a little thing like that embarrass us. I have been thinking about it."

He gazed directly into her eyes. "So have I."

She met his gaze, and suddenly all the discomfort was back. "It's like damming up water," she said, trying for an air of objectivity. "All your—er—masculine energy has been building up, and a little was bound to trickle out when—when—the opportunity arose," she said, blushing.

"A trickle?" he asked, chewing a grin.

"Well, perhaps a little more than that. Will you have some of this plum cake? It looks nice and fresh."

He passed his plate, smiling broadly now. Samantha could not suppress a little laugh as she put a piece of cake on the plate.

He admired her dainty wrist and hand as she poured his tea. A sensation of ease ungulfed Salverton. It was pleasant, sitting chatting with Samantha, taking tea, and forgetting the world for a while, enjoying a little discreet flirtation with a beautiful lady. He hadn't given a thought to politics all day. It would be nice to come home to this relaxing mood at the end of a hard day. It would add years to his life. Gray hairs? He hadn't noticed them.

"How many gray hairs?" he asked.

Samantha laughed. "Vanity, Edward, from you? You're the last man I would suspect of it."

"What do you mean by that?"

"Only that you don't seem to care for such trifles as fashion. Your jackets are well cut, but those small buttons are not in the latest fashion, and your cravats—well!"

"I had this jacket of Weston! He makes all my jackets." From a pattern, the same pattern he had been using for six or seven years.

"I believe it's those few gray hairs that have brought on this concern," she said. "Color them with tea if they bother you. There were only three or four, just at the temples. How old are you anyway? Thirty-eight, thirty-nine?"

"In my thirty-third year."

She blinked in surprise. "A third of a century."

"Don't put it like that! I'm thirty-two."

"Is that all? I had thought you were that age when I saw you at Celine's wedding five years ago." He scowled. "But you had hardly changed when I met you in London yesterday," she added swiftly. "Imagine, it was only yesterday that I called on you. I wager you're sorry I did."

"On the contrary. I'm glad of it."

"I know you will help keep the family name out of court. Lady Louise wouldn't like that."

He ignored the reference to Louise. "I wasn't thinking of the family reputation, actually. I needed to be shaken out of my lethargy." A rueful smile curved his lips. It made him look five years younger. "You're a very good shaker-upper, Sam."

It was the first time he had used her nickname. "If that's a compliment, I thank you. If, as I suspect, it's a setdown, then I am sorry I disturbed your solemnity."

"I didn't say solemnity. I said lethargy."

"You're not in the least lethargic. You're a regular busybody when it comes to other people. You're solemn."

"I stand corrected. Between you and Sykes, I no longer have the bother of thinking for myself. No doubt he will pop up like a genie and tell us what our next step is to be, and we, like good puppets, will do precisely as he says."

Even as he spoke, Jonathon's head appeared through the door of the tearoom. He beckoned to them rather imperatively.

"The chase is on," Salverton said, and throwing a gold coin on the table, he rose and offered Samantha his hand.

Chapter Fourteen

The shadows of evening were lengthening when they went outside. The jostle of daytime pedestrians on the promenade had diminished to a few stragglers. Some shops were closing. In another hour or two, the evening throng would be out, but for the present, everyone there could be clearly seen, and Mr. Fletcher's hulking shoulders were not among the loiterers.

"How did you get rid of Fletcher, Mr. Sykes?" Samantha asked.

"That's not a tale for such tender h'ears as your pearly shells, Miss Oakleigh. Suffice it to say, he'll not bother us for a while."

"I hope you didn't kill him!"

"A man don't die of a drawn cork and a pair of darkened daylights. I did it out of the way of prying eyes, behind the stable at the Mount Pleasant Hotel. He'll live to pester mankind a few years more till Jack Ketch claims him."

"Let us go on to Rusthall Common before he finds us again," Salverton said.

"I took the precaution of taking our carriage to a friendly farmstead I know on the northern edge of town. You don't mind a little stroll on such a fine evening as this, eh?"

"How far is it?" Salverton asked. "We can't ask Miss Oakleigh to walk—"

"Lord love us," Sykes said, laughing, "what harm can befall her with two such stalwarts as me and you to guard her, melord? She's young and frisky. She'll enjoy it."

"I don't mind, Edward," she said.

They set off, keeping a constant look behind them to ensure they weren't followed. At a small chicken farm on the edge of town, Sykes darted behind the hedgerow and came out driving the carriage. The only other vehicle on the road was a donkey cart. They waited to determine the driver wasn't Fletcher, before leaving.

The Laurels was only half a mile farther north. They met a few carriages returning from Rusthall Common, where visitors had gone to view the fantastic Toad Rock. Ere long, they came to a pair of square stone gateposts. The posts lacked an actual gate, but did hold a painted sign proclaiming THE LAURELS, with a sprig of laurel painted below.

Sykes didn't have to be told to draw the carriage to the side of the road. He wasn't such a flat as to be driving up to the door and giving the occupants an opportunity to dart out the back way. He alit and came to speak to Salverton.

"I'll do a reconnaissance for you, melord," he offered.

"You might guard the back door when we go in, in case they make a run for it," Salverton replied.

"H'excellent thinking. I'll make a proper rogue of you yet." He darted up the driveway ahead of them and was back just as Salverton was helping Samantha from the carriage.

"Nobody home, it looks like," he announced. "No lights burning."

"All this for nothing!" Samantha exclaimed.

"We'll have a look while we're here," Salverton said. "At least we shan't be disturbing anyone's sleep at this hour, as we did in Brighton."

"They might have dowsed the lights if they're—er—doing what Wanda does best," Sykes suggested, and received a glare from Salverton. "Don't worry about Miss Oakleigh," Sykes said with a lecherous grin at the young lady. "She didn't come down in the last rain. Farmers' daughters know what critters get up to, eh, Miss Oakleigh?"

Salverton bunched his hands into fists. "Never mind, Edward," she said in a low aside. "He means no harm."

"You will try to remember you're with a lady, Sykes, and keep a civil tongue in your head," Salverton growled.

"Seems to me it's the gent what's h'upset."

On this cocky speech he strutted up the driveway and disappeared behind the back of the house. Salverton, thoroughly irritated, went toward the front door. Bad enough they had made this trip for nothing, without Sykes flaunting his lewdness in front of Samantha. He lifted his fist to hammer at the door, as there was no knocker.

Samantha twitched at his sleeve. "Don't alert her we're here, in case they're in bed," she said. "Never mind scowling like an angry mule, Edward. I'm twenty-two years old. Just try the door and see if it opens."

"If they're upstairs, it is only common courtesy to give them an opportunity to arrange their toilettes before we go barging in on them."

"You're right. And Sykes will catch them if they try to sneak out the back way."

Without further ado, Salverton banged on the door. After a moment he banged again, and again, until it was clear the house was either unoccupied or the inhabitants chose not to answer the door.

When knocking failed, he tried the doorknob and found, to his considerable surprise, that it opened. Darkness had fallen during the interval since leaving the tearoom. Once inside, they advanced into pitch blackness. When Salverton bumped into a table, he felt about and found a tinderbox and lamp. He lit the lamp and held it aloft, looking all around.

They were in a wood-paneled entrance hall with a staircase leading above. Salverton called a few times. Upon receiving no reply, he looked around the hall. An archway opened on to a saloon on the left. A closed door giving on to another room was on the right. A glance showed him the saloon was unoccupied, but a clutter of journals on the sofa table and a wineglass spoke of recent occupancy.

Salverton went to the journal and picked it up. "It's today's *Morning Observer*," he said to Samantha. "They've been here today. London's morning paper wouldn't be here until afternoon, I shouldn't think. They can't have left long ago."

"There's only one wineglass. It might be the caretaker's. Shall we go upstairs and see if their things are here?"

"Very well."

Samantha picked up a lamp and lit it before leaving. Even two lamps did not quite succeed in keeping the menacing shadows at bay. She feared a dark form would fly out at them, or a bullet. There were four bedrooms upstairs. In three of them, the beds hadn't been made up. The bare mattresses, the dusty dressers, and general air of neglect spoke of long disuse. In the largest bedroom, however, the bed had a full complement of bedclothes tumbled in a heap at the end of the bed. A pair of gentlemen's boots stood on the floor by the bed. A soiled shirt and cravat had been thrown onto a chair.

Salverton set his lamp on the dresser and took a quick look through the drawers.

Samantha put her lamp on the bedside table and examined the boots and linen. "These aren't Darren's. You could put two of him in this shirt. Sir Geoffrey's a large man, isn't he?"

"He'd weigh fifteen stone at least."

"These must be his clothes. Have you found anything?"

"Just his spare linens."

She looked at the bed and picked up a nightshirt, also of a large size. "This has been a complete waste of time," she said in exasperation. "Oh, where can Darren be, Edward? I begin to fear Miss Donny is right, and that wretched female has lured him to Gretna Green." Her voice quavered in fear.

When Edward looked at her, he saw her shoulders slumped despondently. Unshed tears glazed her eyes, but it was the trembling of her lips that caused the wrenching inside. He felt his heart twist in sorrow to see brave, lively Samantha so close to tears.

He went to her and put a consoling arm around her shoulders. "Don't fret yourself, my dear," he said softly. "We'll find them."

A hiccoughing sound issued from her throat. She daubed at her eyes with her knuckles. Salverton brought out his handkerchief and wiped her eyes. "Thank you," she said meekly. "I can't ask you to waste any more of your valuable time on this. You have your work and—and Lady Louise."

His arms tightened around her. At that moment the last place he wanted to be was with Lady Louise. "We'll finish what we started," he said.

Samantha looked up, and saw the glow in his eyes. She suddenly felt shy. "That's very kind of you, Edward," she said.

A shadow of a smile moved his lips. He didn't speak, or even move, but just gazed at her a moment. She had the strange feeling they were alone in the universe, just the two of them, together. Not even the ticking of a clock disturbed the silent intimacy. Then he placed a fleeting kiss on her cheek.

"We'll go back to London and try to pick up the trail there," he said. "Wanda must have friends we could talk to."

"Oh, dozens of them! She knows everyone—well, not the sort of people you would know, but she does have friends."

They took up their lamps and returned below stairs. Salverton kept his arm around her waist. Their hips bumped familiarly as they descended. At the bottom of the stairs he looked at the closed door to the right of the entrance hall. On a whim, he opened it and peered into an oak-lined study with a big oak desk holding pride of place beneath the window. In the shadows he nearly missed the most interesting thing in the room. When he saw it, a gasp of astonishment hung on the air. He wasn't sure whether it came from himself or Samantha.

He looked at her, and saw the lamp tremble in her hand. He grabbed it just before it fell to the floor. She clung to him as if he were a raft in a storm.

"Edward! Is he—"

"I'm afraid so," he replied in a hollow voice.

There was no question that Bayne was dead. The quantity of blood on his waistcoat left no doubt, even if he hadn't been sitting as stiff as a statue, his eyes staring blindly at the doorway. He seemed to be looking straight at them.

They backed out of the room and Edward set their lamps on a table. He didn't feel capable of holding on to a lighted lamp.

"Was it Sir Geoffrey?" she asked, staring into the now-dark room.

Edward closed the door. "Yes."

"Oh, Edward, you don't think Darren—"

"We have no proof Darren was here."

"But who else would kill him?"

"We don't know what enemies he might have had."

"We should report it," she said reluctantly.

"Yes, but first I'll get you out of here. I'll take you to a hotel, and hire a carriage to take you to Miss Donaldson. We'd best extinguish these lamps."

He turned the wick down until the flames guttered out, throwing them into utter darkness. Samantha clung to his arm as they headed for the front door. He was just reaching for the knob, when a loud knocking on the door brought them to a halt.

"Would it be Jonathon?" she whispered.

"He's supposed to be at the back door. He wouldn't knock."

Without the necessity of further discussion, they turned and felt their way along the corridor, heading toward the rear of the house, stumbling over tables and chairs and finally banging into a closed door.

A loud voice echoed from beyond the front door. "Open in the name of the law!" Within two seconds the front door was wrenched open.

Salverton's heart pounded in his throat. To his credit, his first concern was for Samantha as he wrestled with the door that had interrupted their flight. For a lady to be caught in such a predicament as this was unthinkable. He also realized it would do himself no good. He found the handle and got the door open just as Bow Street came pounding down the hall after them.

Once they were safe on the other side, Salverton held the door closed as the officer pushed against it.

"A chair!" he whispered to Samantha.

A wan ray of moonlight showed her they were in a dining room. She grabbed the nearest chair. Salverton wedged it under the doorknob, grabbed her hand, and they continued their flight. They soon found themselves in a kitchen. As they made a frantic search for the back door, they heard the chair under the doorknob give way. Footsteps came hounding after them.

"Stop in the name of the law! Stop, or I'll shoot."

"I can't find the bloody door!" Salverton said in a frantic voice.

Even as he spoke, a door opened and a cool breeze entered the room. A sibilant whisper called, "Here, lads, this way!"

"Thank God for Sykes," Salverton said, and pulled Samantha out the door into the yard, slamming the door behind him.

Sykes rammed a rake against the door to impede

the officers' progress. "Follow me," he said, and led them off through a garden, trampling early peas and carrots as they fled. "I've got the lay of the land. Right this way. Watch your step now. Ha-ha."

Salverton thought it a strange time to be laughing, but then, Sykes probably took all this for a prime joke. He didn't know Sir Geoffrey's corpse was in the study.

Sykes led the way, running pell-mell through a meadow, ducking around bushes and an occasional tree. "Watch your step—ha-ha," he called, and vaulted nimbly forward.

Salverton followed. Not realizing why Sykes had suddenly decided to leap like a deer, he fell into the ha-ha, pulling Samantha in behind him. She landed in a heap in his lap, her arms and legs splayed in a most unladylike pose. The bottom of the ditch held a few inches of mud after the spring rains. And to complete his misery, he feared he had twisted his ankle rather badly. It was the perfectly wretched conclusion to a perfectly wretched visit.

As Edward felt the cold mud ooze into his clothing, Sykes's bold face leaned in over them.

"I told you to watch the ha-ha. Lucky I noticed it. When I saw the cows behaving so proper and not eating Sir Geoffrey's clover, I said to myself, "There's a ha-ha hereabouts, and surely enough, there was. Here, take my hand, love." So saying, his long arm extended toward Samantha.

It was the last straw that this upstart should not only come to Samantha's rescue, but suddenly speak to her in this grossly familiar manner.

"Don't touch her or I'll kill you!" Salverton growled.

Sykes grinned. "In a bit of a taking, ain't we,

melord? Best come along before Bow Street decides to join the party."

"Don't be so silly, Edward," Samantha said, and lifted her hand to Sykes, who pulled her out of the ditch in a trice. Edward clambered out after her, unaided. Mud dripped from his jacket and the seat of his buckskins. When he made the error of putting on his hat, muddy water leaked over the brim to trickle down his face and besmatter his cravat. He brushed it away with the back of his hand. At least he could stand on his wrenched ankle. It hurt like the devil, but it wasn't broken.

"Just come along to the carriage, Samantha. Here, take my coat. I don't want you catching a chill," Sykes said. He removed his jacket and put it around her shoulders.

"Oh, thank you, Jonathon," she said, shivering into it. Sykes led her toward the carriage, with Edward limping along behind until Samantha made Sykes wait for him.

"What happened to put you into such a pelter, melord?" Sykes asked. "More than that bit of a tumble, I'm thinking."

"Sir Geoffrey's been murdered," Salverton announced.

Not even this could phase the imperturbable Jonathon Sykes. "Good riddance," said he. "Your brother did it, do you figure, Samantha?" he inquired with no air of condemnation.

"Certainly not."

"Then we'd best get busy and find out who did, eh?"

Salverton drew a weary sigh. He could hardly cut up at Sykes as he wanted to, when he had just saved them from arrest, and would be required to help them out of this predicament.

Samantha noticed that Edward was limping, and began to make a great fuss over him. This did much to ameliorate his mood. He had stopped scowling by the time they were in the carriage and on their way back to Tunbridge Wells.

Chapter Fifteen

At the outskirts of town, Sykes stopped to discuss with melord where he wished to be taken.

"At least we don't have to worry about reporting the death to the constable," Samantha said. "Bow Street knows about it."

"The thing to do," Salverton said, "is to get you home safely, Samantha. I feel it's my duty to stay here and tell Bow Street what I know."

"You won't tell them about Darren!" she said, aghast.

"They already know of Darren's involvement. They questioned you regarding the theft, in London. My hope is to divert their suspicion to—other areas," he said vaguely.

"Wanda has a finger in it, I don't doubt," Sykes threw in, and for once didn't receive a scowl from melord.

"Very likely, and there's Fletcher, as well, who was in the vicinity."

"But how can I go home?" Samantha asked.

"I'll arrange it," Sykes offered at once.

It went badly against the pluck for Salverton to ask Sykes to drive her to London. There was no saying what advantage the scoundrel would take of a helpless lady.

"Lord Salverton will need you here, Mr. Sykes," she said.

"Nay, I didn't mean I'd drive you myself. I can arrange something with a pal."

Conveyance by a "pal" of Sykes's was not what Salverton wished, or was ready to accept.

"I'd rather stay here with you, Edward," Samantha said with a wheedling pout. "I can't go on the public coach in my present state of disarray. They wouldn't even let me into a polite inn to clean up, looking like a scarecrow."

Even in the shadowed carriage he could see she had not fared much better than himself in the ha-ha. Her bonnet was destroyed, her hair tumbling down, and her gown no doubt as dirty as his own buckskins. As Salverton wanted to keep her with him, it didn't take much wheedling to convince him.

"I daresay you're right. It will be for only a day," he rationalized. "We'll ask around and see if Wanda and/or Darren were here. They might have come planning to use The Laurels. They wouldn't have stayed here when they found Sir Geoffrey at his cottage, but we might pick up some word of their destination at a hiring stable. I wonder why Sir Geoffrey did come to Tunbridge Wells at this time." He looked to Jonathon.

"Chasing after Wanda and her lad, very likely. He might have known she brought fellows here in the past. We'll never know for sure, nor does it matter a brass farthing to us. He came, worse luck for him. What you both need is somewhere to wash the muck off yourselves and get into some clean, dry duds," Sykes said.

"Do you have anything to suggest?" Salverton asked.

"That pal I mentioned, Herbie O'Toole. Him and his missus run a rooming house. They won't blink at the condition of your duds. I can get you a good price."

"Never mind the price. Is it decent?"

"Top of the trees. They've had doctors staying there, and a schoolteacher."

"High society, indeed!"

"Aye, it's a flash ken. Herbie does a fair bit of business with priggers and prancers. He can sell you a change of clothes. A sideline, you might say, to change a fellow's looks when he's on the run."

"Charming," Salverton said. "Lead on."

Sykes drove them to a rambling brick rooming house behind the Common. It was rigged up with a deal of crimson draperies and gilt trim and highly ornate, mismatched furnishings from second-hand dealers and estate sales. But it was cleanish, and there was plenty of hot water. The change of clothes was not only vastly expensive, but in poor taste. They regrouped in the gaudy saloon an hour later.

A jacket with wadded shoulders and a pinched waist lent Salverton the raffish air of a racetrack tout. Samantha wore a low-cut emerald satin gown that would have done justice to a demi-rep (and probably had). To tame its exuberance and conceal her bosoms, she wore a patterned shawl about her shoulders.

"That's a bit of all right!" was Sykes's opinion when he saw her. His blue eyes bulged an inch from their sockets. Then he turned to assess Salverton. "You don't look so much like an undertaker in them duds, melord. Very niffynaffy, if I do say so myself. The muslin company will be all over you."

Salverton hardly considered this a compliment, but Sykes meant well, and he accepted it with good grace.

"Was that the only gown O'Toole had?" he asked Samantha. He fully appreciated the effect of the gown. What brought that quick furrow to his brow was the knowledge that every hedgebird they met would also appreciate it.

"No, there was a bright red one as well, but I thought you might not like it," she said demurely. "It was shockingly immodest. What should we do now?"

"Go on the strut on the Pantiles," Sykes suggested. "If Wanda was here, that's where she'd have been. Ask around of the ladies of pleasure."

"I hardly think that's a suitable thing for Miss Oakleigh to do!" Salverton exclaimed.

"Then I'll do it myself, while you take Samantha for a glass of wine at one of the stalls. They play music at some of them in the evenings. She'll enjoy that." With a wink at Samantha, he added out of the side of his mouth, "You'd rather do that than sit here alone, staring at the walls, I fancy."

Their discussion was interrupted by a loud banging on the front door. The clerk left his desk in the hall to answer it. Sykes put his finger to his lips to caution the others to silence. This seemed unnecessary to them, but as usual, Sykes knew what he was about.

"Bow Street!" a loud voice was heard to exclaim. "I have a warrant for the arrest of Jonathon Sykes."

These were familiar words to Jonathon. He looked about the room for a door that wouldn't pitch him into the arms of the law. Finding none, he headed to the closest window and raised it. Before leaping out, he said over his shoulder to Samantha and Edward, "Don't worry about me if I'm caught. I'll not mention you. You two get busy and find out who killed Bayne, or I'm for it."

When the officer entered the room, he took one look at the open window, the curtain blowing in the wind, and ran to it.

"Stop him, Huggans. That's him!" he shouted out the window.

Salverton was ready to claim no man had been in the room with him, but this ruse was futile. Bow Street had another man posted outside. He caught Jonathon as he landed in the shrubbery and clamped him into manacles.

"What is Sykes accused of?" Salverton demanded in his most lofty accent.

"That's none of your concern, mister," the officer replied.

When Lord Salverton spoke, he was accustomed to something more than civility. He made the lowering discovery that when his position in society was unknown, he was nobody. A strange gentleman in an ill-cut jacket putting up at O'Toole's rooming house was paid no heed whatsoever.

"Where are you taking him?" Samantha asked.

The officer ran a disparaging eye over the green satin gown and said, "To the roundhouse, miss. We don't want murderers roaming the streets, eh?"

"Murderer!"

"Aye, Sykes is the villain who killed Sir Geoffrey Bayne this very night."

On this speech, the officer turned on his heel and went to join his confrere by the shrubbery.

"Edward, we must do something!" Samantha said when they were alone. "Couldn't you post bail or something?"

"Not when the charge is murder. Of course I'll testify that he was with me when the murder occurred, but— Actually, he wasn't with us all day. Is it possible Sykes— What did he do while we were in that tearoom? He was gone for some time."

"He has no earthly reason to kill Sir Geoffrey," she said hotly. "The more interesting question is why Bow Street thinks he did, and how they knew where to find him so quickly. Why did they go to The Laurels in the first place? How did they know anything was amiss there?"

"It's possible Sir Geoffrey was in some trouble we know nothing about, but that still doesn't explain why Bow Street should suspect Sykes, and how they knew he was here now. Someone's been following us all the while, and reported to Bow Street."

"Fletcher!"

Edward began pacing the room. He ran a hand distractedly through his hair to aid concentration. "I don't see who else it could be, but what reason had he to kill Sir Geoffrey? Sykes thought it was Wanda he was after, because of some robbery."

"If he discovered Sir Geoffrey had been Wanda's patron, he might have gone to question him and fallen into an argument. Sykes said Fletcher had killed before. There's no saying with a man like that. But, Edward, we can't just let poor Jonathon languish in jail. We must help him."

"Sykes was right. The best thing we can do is get busy and solve this matter. He's in no real danger, Samantha. Naturally, I'll testify as to his alibi if the case comes to trial. If I interfere now, we'll all end up in jail—including you. What we must do is find Fletcher. That will take some doing. If he did kill Sir Geoffrey, he'll have lit out for London or someplace well away from here."

"We'll never find him in London." She sat with her chin propped in her hands, thinking. After a moment she said, "I wager Fletcher is still looking for Wanda and Darren. He thinks we can lead him to them. He might still be lurking about to follow us. If we go to the Pantiles and let ourselves be seen—well, it might draw him out."

"That could be dangerous. I need a pistol. If only Jonathon were here, he'd know where to get one." He didn't notice he'd called Sykes Jonathon, but it did strike him as ironic that he should be regretting the absence of that scoundrel after wishing him at Jericho for two days.

"Your wits are gone begging, Edward. O'Toole will sell you one—at a vastly inflated price."

"Of course!" He went into the hall and told the clerk he'd like to speak to O'Toole about buying a pistol.

"Herbie ain't too pleased that you lot have brought Bow Street down on his head," the clerk said.

"I'll pay handsomely." He drew a wad of bills from his pocket. "Money is no object."

"Ah, well, in that case, take your pick."

He ushered Salverton behind his desk and pulled out the lower drawer, which held an assortment of guns. "Handle them gentle. They're loaded," he said. "Here's a dainty piece. Five guineas." He handed Edward a gun with ivory inlay on the grip.

"Are you sure it works?" He hefted the gun. It seemed well balanced.

"Ho! Do birds fly? Do fish swim? Herbie O'Toole

sell a gun that don't shoot? It would destroy his reputation."

Salverton pulled off a bill, pocketed the weapon, and returned to the saloon.

"That didn't take long!" Samantha said. She examined the pistol.

"Careful! It's loaded."

"Then we're ready to go on the strut."

Edward tucked the gun into his waistband, frowned at her gown, took the shawl and pulled it closely about her, and they were off to the Pantiles.

"What do we do if we see Fletcher?" she asked.

"We lure him to some dark spot and I ask him a few pertinent questions before taking him to the roundhouse."

"Am I to be the bait?" she asked. "If he likes Wanda, I doubt he will care for me."

"In that gown, he'll care, but that was not my meaning. I'll flash a roll of money if he shows up, then stroll into some dark alleyway, where he'll expect to have easy pickings."

"That might work." After a frowning pause she said, "What if he didn't kill Sir Geoffrey?"

"Then this is all a waste of time, and we shall have to find something else to charge him with, to be rid of him."

"It's not easy being a criminal, is it?" she said pensively.

"No, it ain't. Are you having second thoughts about Jonathon as a husband?"

"A husband!" she exclaimed in astonishment. "I never thought of him as a husband, Edward. Merely as my Esmée, or Wanda. I don't see why you gentlemen should be the only ones to have shady friends. Ladies like a little excitement as well."

"Let us hope today's excitement satisfies you for a long time."

They walked on to the Pantiles. The night crowd was out in full force by that time. They made three tours of both sides before settling at one of the groups of tables where musicians were performing. They ordered wine and continued looking around for any sign of Fletcher. After half an hour they moved on to another musical group. By eleven o'clock the crowd began thinning, and there had been no sign of him.

"This is a waste of time," Salverton said. "I'm taking you back to O'Toole's place. I'm going to visit Jonathon. He'll know better than I what to do. My innocent past hasn't trained me for this sort of job."

"I shan't go to bed until I hear from you. Come to my room before you retire."

"Of course. I'll let you know what Jonathon has to suggest."

They returned to the rooming house. Salverton accompanied Samantha upstairs, as there were a few undesirable-looking men in the lobby.

At her doorway he took her two hands in his and said, "I hate leaving you here alone. Don't leave your room if you can possibly avoid it, and don't let anyone in. I'll be back as soon as I can."

"You treat me as if I were a child, Edward. I know better than to mix with people of O'Toole's sort. I've had my taste of the low life, enough to last a lifetime."

"Just when I find myself acquiring a taste for it," he said in jest.

"You be careful, too. Fletch might be lurking about, looking for you."

“He’s not likely to follow me into the roundhouse.”

“No. Well, good-bye, then.”

“Aren’t you going to wish me luck?” His fingers tightened on hers.

“Of course. Good luck, Edward.”

“That is not what I meant,” he said, and drew her into his arms for a kiss.

It wasn’t the wild, out-of-control sort of kiss they had exchanged in the tree tunnel. Samantha was determined not to let that happen again. His lips brushed hers, and as his arms began to tighten and his lips firm, she withdrew.

“Good luck,” she said again, and gently closed the door.

Salverton returned below and got directions to the roundhouse from the clerk. He patted his pistol and went out the door. In his mind was the image of Samantha, reluctantly closing the door. She hadn’t wanted to stop that embrace any more than he had. As he walked along, a random thought of the opera he was missing wafted through his head. What a dull scald it would have been. Much more exciting to be chasing after a murderer. This was real living!

In her room, Samantha locked the door. Then she drew a chair to the window and watched as Edward left for the roundhouse, looking raffish in that horrid jacket. She shook her head to think how he must be hating all this low sort of thing she had dragged him into. Always the gentleman, he tried to hide his displeasure, but he could not like it. Then her thoughts turned to Darren, and the peal she would ring over him when they found him. If they found him.

Chapter Sixteen

"I'd like to see Mr. Sykes," Salverton said to the guard in charge at the roundhouse.

The guard took one look at Salverton's jacket and said, "Hired hisself a fancy lawyer, eh! He must be planning to plead innocent. It do beat all how so much crime gets done, and all the criminals innocent as newborn babes. He'll be up before the magistrate in the morning, but he'll be bound over. Murder's serious. We don't hold with murder in Tunbridge Wells. Bad for the tourist business."

Salverton went along with the misapprehension that he was Sykes's lawyer, as it ensured quick access to the prisoner. He found Sykes playing cards with three other miscreants in a locked room. There was no air of punishment save for the bars on the window and the smoke from the vile-smelling cigar that turned the air blue. The room, he could hardly call it a cell, had a well-battered deal table and four mismatched chairs. Glasses of ale sat amid the cards on the table.

Sykes looked up when he saw Salverton. "Excuse me, lads," he said, and placing his cards facedown on the table, he went off to a corner to speak in private with his caller.

"You shouldn't of come here!" he scolded. "I see

you're surprised at the luxury of the place. The regular cells were full of drunk and disorderly young gents. They had a party that got out of control, so me and the lads were put up here. I was going to send you off a note with my news as soon as the game was over. I'm weaseling the facts out slow like, so as to avoid suspicion."

"News? What have you found out?"

"Smokey Dalton knows Fletch," he said, nodding to the prisoner who was smoking a cigar. "They shared an ale this afternoon, before Smokey forgot hisself and snaffled a jewelry box in one of them shops on the Pantiles and got arrested. Fletch is looking for Wanda, like I thought, but not because she was in on the robbery."

He paused a moment to add a touch of drama to his tale.

"Why, then?" Salverton asked.

"She's his wife." He smiled to see Salverton's eyebrows rise at this stunning announcement. "He was after Bayne and Darren Oakleigh and anyone else that's touched her tender body, if you follow me. Half of London must be trembling in its boots since Fletch hit the streets. Dalton thinks Bayne ran to ground here in Tunbridge Wells when he heard Fletch was out. Since Fletch didn't know where to find him, he went looking for Wanda's latest beau. He learned from Wanda's chums in London that she was seeing Oakleigh, and where he lived."

"You think he followed Miss Oakleigh and me all the way from London to Brighton and on to Tunbridge Wells?"

"I do, and I think as well that Fletch is the reason Wanda was so almighty eager to get out of town in the first place."

"We've been wondering how Bow Street came to drop in at The Laurels so conveniently, and knew you were at O'Toole's as well. You don't think Fletch knew where Sir Geoffrey was hiding?"

"He didn't know when he got here, but he'd find out soon enough. Bayne's an important man. People would know he has a cottage here. I figure when Fletch found out, he left us for a few hours and did Bayne in, then nipped back to town. The Laurels is next door to Tunbridge Wells. It wouldn't take him half an hour. He was coming from the right direction when I saw him and got him behind the stable for a bit of the home brewed. He must have recovered quicker than I figured and picked up our trail. He must of seen us head toward Rusthall Common tonight and figured where we were going. Now, don't take a pet, melord, for the next step is pure conjecture, but my thinking is that he sent Bow Street out to The Laurels, hoping to hang the murder on me, so you and Samantha would be at his mercy."

"But you weren't even in the house. It's myself who would have been arrested if Bow Street had arrived a minute sooner."

"Fletch didn't know that. I was close enough that I'd have been taken in. Fletch may not know your name yet, but he would have seen your fancy ken in London, and know you're above the law. It'd be Jonathon Sykes that was hauled in."

Salverton found this explanation credible. "How did he know you'd be at O'Toole's?" was all he said.

"Where else would I stay in Tunbridge Wells?" was the answer. "Every town of any size has a spot you can go when you're in a bit of trouble, like. In Brighton, the lads stay at my place; in London there's half a dozen spots, but in Tunbridge Wells, we stay at O'Toole's. Fletch likely hung about outside until he saw me go in, then sent a note off to Bow Street. I don't see how else they found me."

This also sounded reasonable. "We've got to find him, Jonathon."

"Aye, for the next number on his list is young Oakleigh, if I know anything."

"Fletch wouldn't stick around here, I shouldn't think. Where would he go?"

"He'll stick to your coattail like a burr till he finds Oakleigh and Wanda. That's my thinking. You may not see him without Jonathon Sykes's eyes to help you, for he's a sly dog, but he'll be after you sure as hanging follows a conviction. What you don't want to do is lead him to young Oakleigh."

"That, at least, is no problem. We don't know where he is. What would you do, Jonathon?"

"I'm accused of robbing Bayne as well as killing him," he said with a cagey look.

Salverton frowned, sensing that he was missing something, but he couldn't for the life of him see how this altered matters.

"Bayne's pocket was to let when they found him," Jonathon said. "Watch gone as well, ring—everything. They searched me when they brought me. Asked me what I'd done with Bayne's watch and ring and money purse. They've had a neighbor in to quiz him. He says Bayne always carried a great gold turnip watch and wore a ring with a red stone. He could identify them. They say he usually carried a wad of blunt as well."

"Yes?" Salverton said encouragingly.

"Lord love me, do I have to draw you a picture?"

"That would help," Salverton said in an unusually humble manner.

"How have you survived so long, melord? You're innocent as Miss Oakleigh. Here's what you do, then. Fletch will be hot on your tail. You send word ahead to Bow Street to be waiting for you out of sight at a safe spot of your choosing. When Fletch comes lurking about, Bow Street hauls him in. He'll not have laid the watch and ring on the shelf, for his pockets are jingling with the blunt he stole off Bayne, see? He hasn't got a place to actually live yet. He'll have the goods in his pocket, for he'd not leave them unguarded in any of the places he's likely to find a safe bed. It'll go a long way toward proving he kilt Bayne. Nobody'd be fool enough to kill a man and leave such treasures behind. Then you step forward and tell the judge I was with you when the murder was done." A worried frown creased his brow. "Do you understand what I'm saying, melord?"

"Yes, I understand. What do you mean by a safe place to trap him, Jonathon? Is O'Toole's safe?"

"O'Toole's? *O'Toole's?*" he asked in a voice high with disbelief. "Lord love me, I'd as soon trust my daughter with the dragoons. I'd not trust O'Toole's. Herbie is all right, but you never know which of his servants Fletch might have in his pocket. Nay, go back to your own bailiwick, someplace where you have people you trust. Your own house, if it ain't beneath your dignity to have Bow Street lurking about the shrubbery to scandalize the neighbors."

Salverton nodded. "My servants are eminently trustworthy. But I don't like to leave you here. I could speak to a magistrate—"

Sykes shook his head firmly. "Nay, Fletch will be

easy in his mind if he don't have me to deal with. Besides, I'm filling my pockets with this set of Johnnie Raws," he added, glancing to the table, where a pile of gold coins at his place indicated a game for deep stakes.

"Well, don't worry about the trial. I'll be there to give evidence."

"Just see you don't get yourself kilt, or I may find myself in a bit of trouble."

"I'll be careful, Jonathon." He felt more gratitude than this was due to Sykes. "If I've behaved badly the past days—and I know I have—I want to apologize. I do appreciate all your help. I don't know what we would have done without you."

"It was a pleasure. Now that we're all friends, I might tip you the clue. You cave in too easy, melord. On money matters, that is to say. I've overcharged you at every turn. It'll be weighing on my mind now that we're pals. I'm too scrupulous, it was ever my failing. I shouldn't ought to have gypped you, but you bled so free, it was too much temptation for a weak man."

A rueful smile curved Salverton's lips. "In my opinion, you've earned every penny, Jonathon."

"Then I've been underpaid all my life. It's been the easiest rhino I ever picked up—save for old Lord Egremont. He was an innocent if there ever was one. Never checked his pockets, nor his wine cellar, nor his wife, come to that. Ah, they don't make them like Egremont no more." He shook his head in fond remembrance. "Away with you now. And take good care of Miss Oakleigh. But then, I don't have to tell you that, do I?"

"No, you don't."

"She's a grand girl. You don't want to let her get away."

"You used to call her Samantha. Why so formal, Jonathon?"

"I figured, for a few hours there, that she might have me if her brother turned out a murderer and thief, but that was just daydreaming. I always had an eye above my station where the ladies are concerned."

"We all dream."

"We'll be in touch soon, melord."

"We will. Thanks, Jonathon, more than I can say."

"My pleasure."

Salverton left, a wiser and a humbler man, and Jonathon returned to his shaved cards to fleece his cellmates.

Salverton kept an eye out for someone following him as he returned to O'Toole's. He couldn't see anyone, but he discerned, or imagined, an occasional soft footstep or rustle in the shadows. He didn't reach for his pistol. Jonathon said Fletch was following him in hopes of finding Darren, and that effectual gentleman would know. Gentleman? Well, one of Nature's gentlemen. Samantha, with a woman's intuition, had sensed it from the first. What a politician he would have made if only he had been born to a higher position in society. Sharp as a bodkin, and not overly burdened with principles.

Before long, Salverton was tapping at Samantha's door. It opened immediately and she beckoned him in.

"How is Jonathon?" she asked.

"Happy as a cow in clover, enjoying a wet and a lucrative game of cards."

"What does he suggest we do?"
"Return to London."
"We can't abandon him, Edward."
"We're not abandoning him. We're now in charge of solving the case. Grab your shawl. We'll hire fresh horses and a driver and be on our way back to London. I'll explain as we go."
Anything could be bought or had if enough money was offered. Within half an hour a driver and team of four swift horses had been hired and they were on their way to London. As they sped through the black night, Salverton outlined his discussion with Sykes, and told her what he planned to do.
"I see you've come to appreciate Jonathon," she said.
"I expect I would have sooner if—well, never mind that."
Samantha had an inkling of his meaning. "You won't want Bow Street hanging about your house," she said. "Send them to Upper Grosvenor Square."
"The influx of my footmen might be noticed. We don't want to tip Fletch the clue. If it's a choice between catching him or letting him go free, I'd gladly invite Bow Street to sit down at my table. This is no time to stand on dignity."
"It's very kind of you, and certainly we must help Jonathon in any way we can, but—" A frown puckered her brow.
"What is it, my dear?"
"But it still doesn't help us find Darren."
"It keeps him alive. We'll find him. Once Wanda learns Fletch has been captured and Sir Geoffrey is dead, she'll feel safe to return to her old haunts again. Darren will turn up."

"That's true. Now that Sir Geoffrey is dead, will the case against Wanda and Darren be dropped?"

"I expect so. Sir Geoffrey can't give evidence that there was any money in his safe to be stolen. They won't take such an uncertain case as that to court. If the Crown does decide to prosecute, which I don't think likely, a sharp lawyer won't have any trouble getting them off. Who is to say the servants didn't take the money?"

The time passed quickly, with so much to discuss. It was after midnight when they reached Seven Oaks. Despite frequent peeks out the window to check for signs of Fletcher, they had not spotted him, but Jonathon said he would be there, and they took it for gospel that he was.

"We'll stop here to give Fletch time to catch us up," Salverton said. "A bite of dinner wouldn't go amiss. That tea and a sandwich several hours ago have worn off."

Seven Oaks was a pleasant little town noted for its fine gardens and Perpendicular Church, but the place of interest to them was an inn. They chose the Royal Crown. Before going in, Salverton had a word with his coachman.

"Keep an eye out for anyone who drives in before we leave, or is loitering about. A big man, dark hair. He might be mounted or in a carriage. Don't accost him, but just let me know if he shows up."

"Right you are, sir."

In the inn, Salverton requested a private parlor. A gray-haired gentleman and his wife were leaving as they were led to the room.

The man stopped and lifted his quizzing glass. "Good God, Salverton, is that you?" he exclaimed. His wife, a portly dame in puce crepe, examined first Salverton's jacket, then Samantha. Her nose pinched in disapproval.

"Lord Urquehart! And Lady Urquehart," Salverton said, and bowed. "May I present my cousin, Miss Oakleigh. We are just on our way to London."

"As are we," Urquehart said, staring at Samantha. "A family funeral at Grinstead," he added.

After saying this, Lord Urquehart was temporarily bereft of speech. What was Lord Salverton doing at an inn with a lightskirt at midnight, and wearing a jacket that was better suited to a counter jumper? Urquehart's good lady was not accustomed to being introduced to lightskirts, and walked on with her nose in the air. Her husband hastened after her.

"What ails them?" Salverton asked, genuinely confused.

"From the way the old goat was staring at me, I should think he made the same mistake as Lord Carnford," Samantha replied. "And that jacket you're wearing didn't help, either."

"Gudgeons," Salverton said, and went into the private parlor. Was it only two days ago he had actually cared about such things? What an ass Sam must have thought him.

Chapter Seventeen

The private parlor was so cozy, the wine and food so good, and especially the company so enjoyable that Salverton was inclined to linger at the Royal Crown. There had been difficulties enough in the Wanda affair that he felt he had earned an hour's relaxation with Samantha. They were both in good appetite, and refrained from spoiling dinner by discussing their predicament.

As they finished their meal, Salverton said, "I'd like to take you to Berkeley Square rather than Upper Grosvenor Square when we reach London, Sam."

"You know perfectly well I can't stay alone with a bachelor," she protested, though she was pleased that he wanted to be with her.

"Of course not. Now that we're returning to civilization, you shall require a chaperon. I'll bring Miss Donaldson to stay with us. She can't be comfortable in that pokey flat with only Mary to look after things."

"I see what it is. You fear Fletcher will decide to stick with me and pester us at Upper Grosvenor Square. I wonder if he will. He might follow you home, since you have the carriage."

"He'll monitor the house where Darren lives.

Why do you think I want you elsewhere, properly guarded? You're Darren's sister. Where is Darren more likely to go? His own house, or mine, when he didn't see fit to call on me during the whole month of your visit." This reminder of their dereliction was accompanied by an accusing look.

"We were sadly remiss in the civilities, but Fletcher doesn't know that."

"Fletcher won't do anything tonight, at least. We should reach London around three-thirty. He'll hire a bed in one of those 'spots' Jonathon spoke of, and be at one or the other of our doors early in the morning."

"You'll call for me?" Something in his expression revealed his reluctance to do so. "Don't think you're going to cut me out just when things are getting exciting. I feel quite sure it's Upper Grosvenor Fletcher will be watching, in any case. If you wish to lure him to Berkeley Square, you must call on me."

"It hardly seems worthwhile going home. I could sleep on your sofa?"

She thought he was joking, but when she looked at him, she saw he was awaiting an answer. "If you could see yourself, you would realize you must go home and change. You don't want the neighbors to see you in that jacket. You look a perfect quiz, Edward."

"A suitable escort for you, Miss!"

"Did you see how Lady Urquehart stared!" she said, and could not quite control a gurgle of laughter. "I fear your reputation will be in tatters. I hope she isn't a bosom bow of Lady Louise's. I cannot think so; she's twenty years older."

Salverton didn't want to think about Lady

Louise. The knowledge that he was expected to propose at the ball that same evening sat like a murky shadow at the back of his mind. He wanted more than anything in the world to marry the beautiful lady beside him. Samantha's shawl had been put aside once she was in the private parlor. Her enchanting shoulders and the swell of her bosoms had proved a great distraction all through Salverton's dinner.

He was beginning to think he would speak to Jonathon about his predicament vis-à-vis Lady Louise, after Sykes was out of jail. This seemed the sort of problem he, with his interest in women, would have encountered. No doubt he was adept at evading parson's mousetrap without offending anyone's feelings.

"They're acquaintances, no more," he replied, and immediately changed the subject. "So I am to deliver you to Miss Donaldson, and call for you early in the morning to take you to Berkeley Square?"

"That would be best. Shall we go now?"

"Let's have coffee. It will keep our eyes open until we reach London."

Samantha yawned into her fist. "I'm not accustomed to such late hours. I was planning to have a snooze on the way home," she said.

It immediately flashed into Salverton's head that she'd sleep with her head on his shoulder. In the dark intimacy of the carriage, he'd put his arm around her.

"A good idea," he said at once, and added, "you need your beauty sleep," for the sole purpose of seeing her delightful *moue*. He placed some coins on the table and called for his carriage. It was drawn up at the inn door, awaiting them when they went out.

Their coachman showed Samantha into the carriage before having a quiet word with Salverton. "That gent you was asking about, sir. A big hulking fellow rode up on a bay mare shortly after you went inside. He sent the ostler into the taproom to bring him an ale. He left ten minutes ago, heading for London."

"Excellent."

"A nasty-looking customer. Are you expecting trouble? If so, I'd ought to try to get hold of a gun."

"I have a gun, but the man won't bother us. He's merely following me in hopes I'll lead him to his quarry."

"If you say so, sir."

Salverton got into the carriage and said to Samantha, "Fletch was here. He went on ahead ten minutes ago. He's riding. He'll duck into some shady spot and wait until we pass, then follow us."

"That's good news, but it makes my flesh crawl to think of him hounding after us in the dark like that." She gave an involuntary shiver.

"You were going to rest," he reminded her.

She peered nervously out the windows. "I'm not sure I can now, knowing he's out there."

"You can use my shoulder for a pillow," he suggested, and moved over to her banquette.

As the carriage lurched into motion, he drew her head onto his shoulder and sat with his arm around her. His quiet smile was invisible in the darkness. Samantha wasn't smiling, but she looked peaceful. She felt safe and snug with Edward's strong arm protecting her. She had hoped he might indicate in some manner that he had decided not to offer for Lady Louise. She sensed, as a woman in love does, that he truly cared for herself, but obviously he felt committed to Lady Louise. He was too fine a gentleman to slip off on her if some commitment had been implied by his behavior.

She was visited by a forlorn wish that she had gone to Edward when they first arrived in London. He would have led her and Darren to more worthy companions than they had found by themselves. She would have been spared all this worry over Darren, yet some good had come of it. Edward had been shaken out of his crippling propriety and stuffiness. But would the new Edward be happy with Lady Louise? Eventually, her eyelids fluttered shut and she fell into a light doze.

Salverton enjoyed the drive. His chest swelled in tenderness as his fingers twined in Samantha's silky curls and stroked the vulnerable nape of her neck. Her shoulders glowed like marble in the wan ray of moonlight that penetrated the carriage. They were not cold and hard like marble when his palms held them, however. They were warm and soft and smooth as velvet. At times he caught a glimpse of her bosoms, rising and falling as she slept. They provided a nearly irresistible temptation.

As he gazed at her sweet face, gentle in repose, he knew this was no mere fascination. He had grown to love his cousin, not in spite of her rusticity and hoydenish ways, but because of them. If society thought he had chosen his bride poorly, then society could go to the devil.

While they drove along, a bulky man with a hat pulled low over his eyes dogged them like a shadow. Fletcher was so accomplished in his chosen trade that they didn't notice when he rode out from under a stand of willows and began following them. He rode on the very edge of the road, invisible in the shadows of night.

Salverton didn't awaken Samantha until the carriage stood in front of her house on Upper Grosvenor Square. He was tempted to awaken her with a kiss, but before he had quite made up his mind to it, the coachman was at the door. The sound of the door opening awoke her. She looked all around, blinking in confusion. A tousle of curls framed her sleepy face. This is how she would look when she awoke beside him in the morning.

"Oh, we're home already. Have you seen Fletcher?" she asked.

"No, but there's no reason to think we've lost him. I expect he's waiting around the corner."

"You will call for me in the morning, Edward. Promise! I want to be there when you spring the trap on Fletcher."

"I'll call for you at nine."

"That late? You don't think—"

"You need a good night's rest. And so do I."

He assisted her from the carriage and accompanied her into the house, up to the door of their flat. Samantha had her key and let herself in quietly. She didn't light any lamps, as she planned to go directly to her bedroom.

"I shan't waken Auntie," she whispered. "There's no reason she must know at what ungodly hour we returned."

"You might take a look in Darren's room, in case he came back during our absence."

"Yes, that's a good idea."

When he heard the eagerness in her voice, he was sorry he'd said it. Suggesting Darren was at home had been only a ruse to get inside to kiss her good night.

Salverton stepped in. She lit a lamp then and tiptoed silently down the hall to Darren's room. She could see from the doorway that his bed was empty, and her hopes fell. Her shoulders were sagging when she returned to the hallway.

"He's not here. I wonder where he's sleeping tonight. If he has the faintest notion what's going on, he must be frightened half to death."

"Wanda might have told him about Fletch, to put him on his guard."

"I warrant she didn't mention that he's her husband. At least there's no danger of Darren being married to her. Even if she did convince the gudgeon to flee to Gretna Green, the wedding wouldn't be legal. It would be horrid for him to make such a misalliance, having to live his whole life with a woman who doesn't suit him, and a bossy, bullying woman besides. He would soon stop loving her."

She didn't realize the words might apply equally to Edward and Louise until they were out of her mouth. She came to a conscious pause and looked at him, half apologetically, half questioningly. If he was ever going to declare he had changed his mind about Lady Louise, surely he would do it then.

"A marriage would be a wretched mistake," he said with warm feelings but with no air of taking the remark personally. "They have nothing in common. She'd run through his fortune within a year. It's a pity he was ever caught in her snare, but I'll say no more about why that happened."

His quizzing smile, of course, referred to their not calling on him until the damage was done. As Salverton had no intention of marrying Lady

Louise, he didn't see any reference to his own situation in her remark. Just how he was to disentangle himself from Louise was unclear. He took some relief in the knowledge that he had never actually proposed. At least fate had prevented him from that final error. He foresaw a gradual cooling of the relationship and regretted the necessary weeks or months before common decency would allow a marriage to Samantha.

"You had best go now," she said. "Thank you for everything, Edward. You've been so very helpful."

He studied her unhappy face. His gaze lingered a moment on her shadowed eyes and her full lips before sliding down to her white shoulders. When his arms began to reach for her, Samantha didn't pull back. It was the way he was looking at her that held her immobile. If that wasn't love . . . The breath caught in her lungs. Was he going to say it now, that he had changed his mind about Lady Louise? A hush gathered about them. No actual words were spoken, but some vital knowledge seemed to hang in the air.

Into the silence a querulous voice penetrated, shattering the mood.

"Is that you, Samantha?" It was Miss Donaldson. Her head and shoulders appeared around the corner. The shoulders were covered in a blanket.

"Yes, it's me."

When Miss Donaldson saw Lord Salverton, all but her head disappeared. It wouldn't do for Cousin Edward to see her wearing a blanket for a negligee. "You're very late," she scolded. "I expected you hours ago."

"We ran into a deal of—unexpected happenings."

"Any word on Darren?"

"Edward is just leaving. I'll tell you all about it. You haven't heard from Darren?"

"Just a note, delivered by a ragamuffin street lad telling us not to worry. He is all right."

"A note!" Samantha and Edward exclaimed in unison.

"I'll be right out to show it to you."

Miss Donaldson disappeared to make herself decent. In the interest of speed, she just put her street mantle on over her nightdress and brushed her hair. Samantha pulled the patterned shawl tightly around her shoulders to hide the green satin gown. She had hoped to dispose of it before meeting Miss Donaldson. The chaperon returned to the saloon and handed Edward the note. It was a ragged piece of paper torn from the corner of a journal.

"When did this come?" he demanded.

"About six o'clock in the evening. I quizzed the lad who brought it. He said a man had handed it to him in Hyde Park and gave him a crown to deliver it. And promised I'd give him another to make sure he did bring it. The description of the man sounded like Darren. The writing is certainly his, though one can see he was distressed when he wrote it."

In her eagerness to read the note, Samantha went to peer over Edward's shoulder. " 'Dear Sam and Miss Donny, Don't worry about me. I'm fine, but I can't join you at the moment. You go on home to Oakbay. I'll see you there within a week.' "

"How does he think we are to go home with no carriage and no money?" Miss Donaldson inquired in a rhetorical spirit.

"Of course we shan't go home without him,"

Samantha said. She looked to Edward. "Do you think he's all right?"

"I suspect he knows very well that Bow Street is after him, or why wouldn't he come here? Fletcher wasn't on his tail. He's been following us."

"Who is Fletcher?" Miss Donaldson asked. As the excitement abated, she noticed that Sam wasn't wearing the gown she had left in. Nor did Salverton look at all his usual elegant self. "And what happened to your clothes?" she added in confusion.

The lengthy explanations were made as brief and innocent as possible, which still left plenty of occasion for Miss Donaldson to lift her eyebrows and exclaim in bewilderment. Between their driver being locked up in jail for murder and the pair of them apparently purchasing worn clothing from an inn that did not sound at all the thing and their being followed home by a jailbird, one could not help wondering if she had been remiss to let Samantha go alone with her cousin.

"Wanda married the whole time, and to a thieving murderer. I never heard of such a thing," she said weakly after the tale was told. Had Samantha's companion been anyone but Cousin Edward, she would have said a good deal more.

"I made sure it was Sir Geoffrey that Darren was trying to hide from," she said a moment later. "Dead, imagine that! One must pity him, but there's no need for hypocrisy. Decent men don't get murdered in their own homes. The man was a lecher, when all's said and done. His death makes the matter of the stolen thousand pounds a little less dark for Darren. How are we to find him?

Should we go to Hyde Park tomorrow to look for him?"

"We don't want to lead Fletcher to him," Edward said. "Jonathon suggests we lure Fletcher into a trap. I've chosen Berkeley Square as the safest place." He outlined Sykes's suggestion.

The only thing more shocking than Edward's taking counsel from a jailbird like Sykes was that Edward was willing to use his own home for such a low purpose. It could only be love that was leading him so far from his usual stodgy path. And doing it all with such carefree abandon, almost as if he were enjoying it.

"So you hope to entrap Wanda's husband tomorrow morning. I hope your plan succeeds, Cousin. Most kind of you to look out for our interest in this manner. Of course you will let us know at once when he has been apprehended," Miss Donaldson added.

"I plan to be there," Samantha said. Before her chaperon could object, she added, "I am a necessary part of the plan, Auntie. Edward thinks Fletcher will be hovering about here at Grosvenor Square. You would not feel safe with him on your doorstep. Edward will call for me and we'll lure him into the waiting hands of Bow Street at Berkeley Square."

"I'll see that nothing happens to Sam," Edward assured her. Sam! The romance had obviously progressed nicely.

"If you say so, Cousin," she said meekly, and lowered her head to conceal the triumphant gleam that entered her shrewd eyes. "At least there is no need to worry about Darren. We know he is safe."

"Or was when he wrote this," Samantha said. "One can only hope Wanda hasn't put him on to those 'spots' Jonathon spoke of. It would be fatal if Darren and Fletcher ended up in the same hidey-hole."

"I wish I had asked Jonathon where these hiding places are in London," Edward said. "I could make a tour of them now. We could use Jonathon's expertise, could we not?"

"Now you appreciate him," Samantha said with a saucy smile.

"We appreciate different aspects of Jonathon. You were taken in by his handsome phiz; it is his expertise that I admire. And his eagerness to help. If he were here, he'd make the arrangements at Bow Street for me, and save me that trip before I go home tonight."

"Poor Edward," she said with a teasing smile.

Miss Donaldson considered retiring to her room. But no, she must keep some shred of common decency in the proceedings. She stuck like a barnacle until Salverton eventually took his leave. She was the only one who was smiling as she went to bed. Cousin Edward was certainly in love with Samantha. A blind man would know by the heat coming from him that he was scarcely able to control himself. It would certainly come to a match—if only Darren didn't ruin it in some manner. Any public humiliation of Darren might be enough to cool Cousin Edward's fire. The future at Oakbay would be gloomy indeed with a heartbroken Samantha to deal with as well as a disgraced Darren.

Samantha was less hopeful. Edward hadn't said a word that indicated he meant to jilt Lady Louise. The very word would be anathema to him. She worried, too, that Darren and Fletcher might end up in the same disreputable rooming house that night, but only one of them would walk out of it in the morning.

Salverton, being in charge of the operation, tried to keep his mind on business. After they caught Fletcher would be time to consider the future. At Bow Street, Townsend came up with the notion of having Sykes brought under guard to London at once to assist him with the case.

"The easiest way of getting him out of jail. It avoids a deal of paperwork," he explained.

After Salverton had made all the arrangements with Bow Street and was lying in his own bed, he did allow himself a period of joyful contemplation of life after Wanda.

Chapter Eighteen

The neighbors had no cause to complain of Lord Salverton's toilette the next morning, whatever of his activities. He looked unexceptionable in an exquisitely cut jacket of blue superfine when he climbed into his carriage at a quarter to nine. The cravat at his throat was more fashionably arranged than was his wont, and his curled beaver sat at a more dégagé angle, but such details were not noticed at a glance. The only divagation from the ordinary was the hour of his departure. He didn't usually call for his carriage until nine-thirty, for the trip to Westminster.

He didn't drive directly to Upper Grosvenor Square, but around the neighboring streets first, trying to spot Fletcher. When he espied the hackney cab loitering at the corner of Culross Street, he stopped a moment to make sure he was seen. When the hackney followed his carriage at a discreet distance, he felt certain it held Fletcher.

Samantha was so eager to see Edward that she was waiting at the window. Fletcher, being a block behind, escaped her notice. She met Edward at the door.

They looked at each other in the uncertain but acutely conscious way of undeclared lovers, each remarking that the other had made a special toilette. Edward thought Samantha looked particularly fetching in a simple sprigged muslin that she regretted having to wear, as her better gowns had been packed off to Oakbay. She noticed Edward looked more dashing than usual.

"I see you've dispensed with the green gown," he said after they had exchanged greetings.

"Miss Donny threw it in the dustbin, but Mary retrieved it." After a brief pause she said, "Has it all been for nothing, Edward? I didn't see any sign of Fletcher."

His smile gave her heart. "He's taking some pains to remain unseen, but I spotted his rig at the corner. Where's Miss Donaldson?"

"She's with Mary. I'll say good-bye to her."

The hopeful chaperon had decided to give the two a moment alone, but she was not so neglectful of her duties that she was in the kitchen. She was listening from her bedchamber and joined them without being summoned.

"Is Bow Street ready to pounce?" she asked Edward.

"They have my place surrounded with men disguised as gardeners and postmen and footmen cleaning the neighbors' brass door knockers. Townsend himself is in my saloon with his eye glued to the street. I doubt a fly could slip through the net. Bow Street has been extremely obliging. Townsend feels Fletcher cheated Jack Ketch the last time he was in court, and is determined to get him this time."

"Then you'll be going directly to Berkeley Square."

"Yes, we're off," Samantha said. "Wish us well."

Miss Donaldson gave her charge a little hug. "Good luck," she said. "You'll let me know at once—"

"Of course. And you let us know if you hear from Darren."

"Don't let him go to Berkeley Square if he should turn up," Salverton added.

"You'd best not tell him what is afoot, or he will come," Samantha added.

"I'll not say a word," Miss Donaldson promised.

While this was going forth, Darren Oakleigh was sitting in the public dining room of a derelict inn in Cheapside. A man who had passed out in a drunken stupor the night before sat across from him with his head on the table. The inn was not one of the "spots" Jonathon Sykes would have recommended, but it was out of the way. Bow Street hadn't found him, at least.

Darren was completely disenchanted with Wanda Claridge. She had led him a merry chase, pretending she wanted to marry him. But halfway to Gretna Green she had changed her mind, and decided she wanted to go to Ireland instead. Ireland, of all places, when his ancestral home was in Wiltshire! How could he tend to Oakbay from Ireland?

It was the thousand pounds that had made her so unbiddable. He wished she had never seen that thousand. Once she got her hands on it, she became very independent.

"Now, see here, my girl, I'll not go to Ireland, and that's that," he had told her.

So she lit out without him, and she wasn't headed for the west coast to catch a ship to Ireland, either. She took the stage back to London. He had checked up, wondering if he should follow her and try to change her mind. He had returned to London, not exactly following Wanda, but once he arrived, he did call on a few of her friends—and it was as well he had.

Wanted by Bow Street for thievery! She had stolen that thousand pounds from Sir Geoffrey Bayne. When Darren had said, "Surely her own cousin wouldn't set Bow Street on her?" Liz Eaton had laughed out loud.

"Cousin, is it? Dutch uncle, more like. She was his mistress. Sir Geoffrey's set Bow Street on the pair of you. You're wanted by the law, mister."

"But I didn't take the money!"

"You was with her. You're an assessory. You'll be lucky to get away with five or ten years. Keep your head down, mister. It ain't only Bow Street you must watch out for, either. Fletch got out last week."

"Out of where? And who the devil is Fletch?"

That was the final betrayal. Wanda was married, and to what sounded like an extremely ugly customer who was jealous as a green cow of his wife and had sworn to "get" anyone who had touched her. Things had gone straight downhill from there. It seemed Fletch knew that he had been seeing Wanda, and was coming after him. Darren had no idea what had happened to Wanda. She was likely hiding out somewhere. Who could blame her? Perhaps she had decided to go to Ireland after all. That was fine for Wanda, but what was to become of him? He couldn't spend the rest of his life lurking about such dens as this.

He daren't go back to Upper Grosvenor Square. Wanda's friends might have given Fletch that address. Liz had let him know you gave Fletch whatever he wanted if you knew what was good for you. He couldn't go to Bow Street for help, or he'd end up in Newgate. He had nowhere to turn, including Oakbay. Fletch would have that address as well. He couldn't have the scoundrel near Oakbay, pestering Sam and Miss Donny.

He sat staring into a greasy mess of uneaten gammon and eggs, occasionally taking a sip of the turbid brew they called coffee. What could he do? Where could he turn for help? He knew what Miss Donaldson would say. "Speak to Cousin Edward. He's extremely well connected. He knows everyone who matters." P'raps Salverton knew a good lawyer. Darren was beginning to think a lawyer was his best bet, but good ones didn't come cheap, and Wanda had pretty well cleaned him out.

He'd have the expense of hiring a hackney to get there. The inn wouldn't let him take his rig out until he'd paid his account. The rattler and prads were being held hostage for his bill. It might be safer in a hired cab anyway, in case Fletcher had a description of his carriage and team.

Salverton was family. He'd lend him the blunt to settle his account here at the inn, and hopefully give him a bed until it was safe to be seen in public. He'd go to call on Salverton. He had a mansion on Berkeley Square, as Miss Donny never tired of reminding them. Darren had visited it once years before with his papa. He didn't remember much about it except that it was the biggest house on the street. He laid a few odd coins on the table, all the money he had left after Wanda's depredations on his purse. Hardly even enough to hire a cab. He'd walk halfway there. No, better to get a drive halfway there, and walk through the more civilized part of London. Fletcher would hesitate to attack him in the polite West End.

Fletcher was wise and well experienced in the ways of tailing a victim. He remained a block and a half behind Salverton's carriage. As it wended its way southeast, he assumed Salverton was taking Miss Oakleigh to his own mansion. The lady'd be better entertained there than in those few rooms on Upper Grosvenor Square, while his lordship continued looking for Darren. Fletch decided to drive along Bruton Place, down Bruton Lane, and meet his lordship when he came out to continue his search.

Darren Oakleigh was somewhere in the city, and sure as God made oaks and acorns, his high-and-mighty friends would be looking for him. It was just at the corner of Bruton Lane and Hay Hill that Fletcher spotted the young fellow scuttling along, looking over his shoulder as if afraid he was being followed.

He assessed the fellow against the description he had gotten from Wanda's friends. A handsome young man, tall, well set up, with chestnut hair. It couldn't be a coincidence that this lad matching the description, and frightened to death into the bargain, was legging it toward his lordship's mansion. So this was the jackanapes that had dallied with his wife. An unlicked cub, still wet behind the ears. Wanda always had a colt's tooth in her head. He'd just wait a minute and see if the lad turned right at the corner. Because if he did, he was going to Berkeley Square—and he must be Darren Oakleigh. Fletch smiled to think of beating the whelp to a pulp with his bare hands. A bullet was too good for him.

At the corner, Darren looked right and left. He was on Berkeley Street, but was Berkeley Square north or south? He hadn't seen Berkeley Square as he came up from Piccadilly, so it must be north. He turned north, and almost immediately the hackney cab drew up alongside him.

Darren had no definite description of Fletcher. "An ugly customer" was all Liz had said, but if ever there was an ugly customer, the man looking at him from the carriage window was it. He looked more like an animal than a man. A bull, with a bull's massive neck and heavy, sloping shoulders. He had a mat of shaggy hair sticking out from under his hat and the most ferocious eyes Darren had ever seen. There was murder in those eyes. Darren took to his heels before the man said a word. The carriage door flew open and the man came hounding after him. Darren was lighter and in better condition. He ran, his heart hammering in his throat, up the west side of Berkeley Square. The bull didn't overtake him, but he didn't fall behind, either.

The footman polishing Lord Montroy's brass knocker heard the pounding feet. He dropped his rag and joined in the chase. A postman suddenly came down the staircase of the house next door. He dropped his bag and joined in. Within seconds there were five men following Darren. He didn't stop to count them, but he could hear the flying feet and the shouts ringing after him. Curious faces appeared at windows. Berkeley Square had not seen such excitement since a mounted policeman had ridden his horse up the steps of Lansdowne

House in pursuit of a highwayman in the last century.

Darren felt that all of London was after him. It was some sort of trap. Bow Street had discovered that Salverton was his cousin, and figured out that he'd go to Cousin Edward for help. It was all over, but at least he'd try to make it to Salverton's door. His cousin might hire him a lawyer. But which house was it? There! The yellow brick one, the biggest, grandest house on the street.

He went, gasping, up to it. As he reached the steps leading to the door, Fletcher tackled him. He caught him by the ankles and brought him to the ground just at the foot of a plane tree. At the same moment, the door flew open and Cousin Edward came out, brandishing a pistol. A swarm of footmen, postmen, and gardeners rolled about on the grass. Curses and imprecations rang on the air.

"I arrest you, Mortimer Fletcher, in the name of the law," the postman declared.

"Here, that's my ankle, ninnyhammer!" a gardener exclaimed, shaking his foot free of the postman's clutches.

"Hands off, Williams. He's mine!" the footman said. "I get the reward for this one!" The footman clamped a set of manacles on Fletcher and said, "He's mine, lads. You can run along now."

"Bring him inside. Townsend is waiting," Edward said, then he turned to Darren. "Oakleigh? Yes, I recognize you. You'd best come in as well."

"Cousin Edward?" Darren asked in a trembling voice. He rose, brushing dirt and grass from his trousers. "I say, I'm sorry about all the commotion. I'm in a spot of trouble. You wouldn't happen to know a good lawyer . . ."

Salverton had intended to ring a peal over Oakleigh, but when he saw the fear and shame on his youthful face, he remembered that long-ago spring of his own folly, and his heart softened. "We'll speak about this inside," he said, and accompanied Darren to the door.

Samantha ran to greet them. She threw her arms around her brother. With tears streaming down her cheeks she said, "Darren, you gudgeon! We've been looking all over for you! Where have you been?"

"Sam, what are you doing here?"

"Where else should I go for help but to Edward? Are you all right?"

Edward smiled ruefully at them, then went to join Townsend.

"I will be when I've caught my breath," Darren replied.

"Where have you been all these days, and what have you been doing?"

"Hiding, of course. That brute, Fletcher, has been looking for me. He's Wanda's *husband*, Sam. Can you beat that? She was married all the time. What a take-in. No wonder she wouldn't go to Gretna Green with me." He peered into the saloon that would have held a couple of his tenant cottages had it not been full of well-polished furniture. "I say! Cousin Edward does pretty well for himself, don't he?"

"We should have come to him in the beginning. He's really very nice."

"More civil than I expected. But tell me what you're doing here."

"First I must let Miss Donny know we found you. I expect she'll want to come here."

Samantha sent the message to Upper Grosvenor Square, then she led her brother to the morning parlor. While Salverton arranged matters with Townsend, Darren and his sister brought each other up-to-date. Salverton joined them half an hour later.

"You'll have to come down to Bow Street with us to answer some questions, Oakleigh," he said.

"If it's about the thousand pounds, I swear I had no notion it was stolen, Cousin."

"It's not about that. That charge will be dropped now that Sir Geoffrey is dead."

"I hope they don't think I killed him!"

"We'll get the whole story from Fletcher. You'd best come along."

Darren rose reluctantly and went toward the door. Salverton turned to Samantha. "You notified Miss Donny?"

"Yes, she should be here soon. Thank you, dear Edward, for everything." She stood on her tiptoes and placed a chaste kiss on his cheek.

He smiled at her, rubbing the back of his fingers along her cheek. It was a small gesture, but intimate, the sort of thing a lover might do without even realizing he was doing it. She wondered if he had ever done it to Louise.

"I'll put in a word for Darren at Bow Street," he said. "If we could find Wanda, it would help clear his name. About the murder, I mean. Townsend will send men out looking for her."

"Did they not find Sir Geoffrey's watch and ring on Fletcher?" she asked in alarm.

"No, but perhaps they're at whatever hole he spent the night in. He's a tough bird. The questioning will take some time. Don't worry, my dear. Things will work out."

"How long will you be gone?" she asked with a woebegone look.

"I'll be back as soon as I can. You'll stay here?"

"Yes, I'll wait for you."

A small, satisfied smile curved his lips. "Good." Then he left.

Chapter Nineteen

At Berkeley Square, the ladies were served tea in the morning parlor to ease their vigil. Noon came and went and still there was no sign of Darren and Salverton returning. There was a deal of hand wringing and worrying about what would befall Darren.

"If only we could find Wanda," Miss Donaldson said not for the first time. "She need not fear coming forward now. She could say Sir Geoffrey gave her the thousand pounds, and who is to say he didn't, when the man's dead."

"We can't ask her to lie, Miss Donny."

"Much it would bother her. When did the hussy ever tell the truth? We don't want any cloud hanging over Darren's head. There will always be rumors if this matter is not cleared up."

"I'm more concerned they'll try to involve him in the murder. Pity they hadn't found the watch and ring in Fletcher's pocket. She could prove Darren was with her when Sir Geoffrey was killed. I could go and visit some of her friends. If I tell them Fletcher is arrested, they might talk to me."

"Stay away from that crew." After a moment's consideration she added, "What you might do, however, is drop a line to that Liz Eaton that Wanda was so close to and ask her if she has any idea where Wanda is."

As Samantha didn't really want to leave the house, she wrote the note and had one of Salverton's footmen deliver it. Another hour passed. Fresh tea and sandwiches were brought to the morning parlor. At two o'clock there was a sound at the front door. Samantha pelted into the hall just as Salverton and Darren came in. She knew by their smiles, and, of course, by Darren's being here and not in jail, that things had gone well.

"What happened?" she asked.

"They found the watch and ring in Fletcher's coat," Darren said. "He had them in the pocket of his greatcoat, which he left in the hackney when he chased me. One of the Bow Street officers thought to quiz the driver. That pretty well convicts Fletcher. Townsend says they've got him right and tight this time. And with Sir Geoffrey dead, the other charge will be dropped, so I am free."

"Oh, thank God!" Samantha said, and threw her arms around her brother. In an excess of relief, she also hugged Edward. His arms closed tightly around her, but as Miss Donaldson chose that moment to come into the hall, he couldn't take full advantage of the situation.

"What news?" Miss Donaldson demanded, and was told. There were tears of joy in her eyes as they all went into the saloon to celebrate with champagne.

They were enjoying a celebratory drink when the door knocker sounded again. "That might be Liz—or even Wanda," Samantha said. "I dropped Liz a note before I knew you had found the watch and ring, Edward. I asked her to send Wanda here if she could find her. I hope you don't mind."

Salverton nodded his approval. "Show the caller in here, Luten," he said to his butler, who had come to inquire whether his lordship was "at home" to callers.

Edward looked with considerable interest to see Wanda—or even Liz, if that was who was calling. He was shocked to look up and see Lady Louise staring at him from her icy blue eyes.

"I see you're busy, Salverton," she said, her gaze sweeping across his company in a condemnatory way. "I should have dropped a note before calling. Did you realize the prime minister's been trying to get hold of you? He's awaiting some important report. I expect it was the commotion here that caused the delay. I heard from Shelburne, your neighbor, there were some strange goings-on here this morning. An arrest, was it? I hope you weren't burgled."

"No. Bow Street used my house as a base of operation to catch a murderer."

Lady Louise's pinched nostrils made clear she disapproved, but she didn't say so. Her steely gaze turned to Samantha. "Mrs. Oakleigh, is it not? I believe we've met before."

"Delighted to meet you again, Lady Louise," Samantha lied. Lady Louise had been much on her mind the past days. Examining her now, Samantha felt she would be the worst thing that could happen to Edward. With this ice maiden by his side, he would revert to his stiff-rumped ways, and forget to enjoy life.

Miss Donaldson opened her lips to correct the

impression that Sam was Mrs. Oakleigh. Seeing her, Salverton leapt into the breach.

"My manners are gone begging," he said. "You've already met Mrs. Oakleigh, Louise. Allow me to present her chaperon, Miss Donaldson, and her husband, Mr. Oakleigh. I would like you all to meet Lady Louise St. John."

Darren frowned and said, "Eh?" as he looked around for Mrs. Oakleigh, his wife.

Lady Louise had not the keenest nose in London, but she smelled something fishy here. Everyone in the room save herself seemed to be on nettles.

It was Miss Donaldson who said, "This is *Miss* Oakleigh, milady. Samantha isn't married. She's Darren's sister."

Salverton received a cool stare from Lady Louise. "Indeed!" she said.

Before she could say more, there was another clatter at the front door. The butler, knowing his lordship was "at home," decided to show the young female in. He would not normally have admitted a female of this sort by the front door, but today was not an ordinary day. She said she had been sent for. The butler assumed she was involved in young Oakleigh's fracas, and accompanied her to the saloon.

"Miss Claridge," he announced.

Salverton stared at a female who could not possibly be younger than thirty-five, though a quantity of rouge and powder lent her cheeks a more youthful hue. She was attractive in a vulgar way, with flashing brown eyes and full lips. Her shapely figure was encased in a lutestring gown of peacock blue and a bonnet trimmed with enough feathers to outfit a whole aviary.

Lady Louise was beyond speech. She could only stare from this vision to Salverton's unmarried cousin, who had certainly claimed to be married, and looking for her husband. She remembered it perfectly.

Ere long, she noticed that the female in peacock blue had every earmark of a lightskirt. She was the female who had been seen in Salverton's carriage the night he chose to miss her dinner party! "Obviously of the muslin company" was the way Carnford had described her. "Pretty as can stare, but not quite the thing." Salverton was trying to fool her that it was this Samantha Oakleigh, his cousin in distress, who had been with him, but she felt in her bones it had been no one else but Miss Claridge.

Wanda looked at the assembled group and said, "You wanted a word with me, Sam? Is it true Bow Street has got Fletch locked up?"

"Yes, it's true," Samantha said, cool as a cucumber. Lady Louise gasped and clutched at her throat. After one quick glance at her, Samantha decided against introducing Wanda to Lady Louise. Rude as it was not to, she feared it would be even ruder to do it, and might cause a heart attack besides.

"Good! That's the last time he'll darken my daylights," Wanda said. "So what did you want with me?" She strolled in and took a seat across from Lady Louise.

"We hoped you might give Darren an alibi for last night," Samantha replied. "As they already have evidence against Fletch, I daresay it won't be necessary now. But thank you for coming."

"I don't mind. I've always wondered what these castles are like inside." She gazed around the room.

"Mighty fine. Is that champagne?" she asked as her wandering gaze fell on the wine.

"Remiss of me. Won't you join us, Miss Claridge?" Edward said, and poured her a glass. "I expect you and Darren would like to talk in private." His intention was to shuffle Wanda off to another room before she became too loquacious.

"I have plenty to say!" Darren said, jumping up. "How's your *husband*, Wanda?"

"You tell me," Wanda replied, and took a sip of the wine. "You've seen him. I haven't, not since they locked him up some years ago. But I'll attend his hanging—with pleasure."

"You never told me you were married!"

"You never asked."

"You might have mentioned it when we was on our way to Gretna Green." Wanda shrugged. "I have nothing more to say to you," Darren said, and turned his head aside.

The audience had been listening attentively.

"Well, that's that," Salverton said. His eyes were twinkling and his lips were unsteady. "May I accompany you to the door, Miss Claridge?" He put his hand in his pocket and rattled some coins enticingly. Wanda drank her wine and rose.

"Ever so nice to meet you. See you around, Sam." She was just picking up her beaded reticule, when the door knocker sounded once more.

Running over the dramatis personae of the drama, Salverton said, "I expect that will be Jonathon."

"Oh, dear!" Samantha said with a glance at Lady Louise.

"Mr. Sykes," Luten announced, and Jonathon pounced into the room, smiling from ear to ear.

"They let me out of jail," he announced. Lady Louise took one look at him and wedged herself tightly against the back of her chair. "Townsend sprung me when you sent word I was with you and Sam when old Bayne was done in, melord. Hello, Sam. This would be your little brother, the cause of all the mischief. Stay away from the muslin company, lad. You're too young for it yet. Take it from one who knows." As he spoke, his eyes wandered to the choice piece in the peacock suit. "Nancy! I didn't expect to see you here."

Lady Louise peered around for another lightskirt, but finally realized that Wanda also wore the name Nancy. Jonathon's glance strayed often to Wanda while Salverton briefly outlined what had occurred since he and Jonathon had parted company in Tunbridge Wells.

"You've kept yourself busy, I must say, melord," Jonathon said. "And handled the affair as well as I could have myself."

"I only followed your orders," Salverton replied. "How did things go in the roundhouse?"

Jonathon drew out a thick wad of bills. "A fair night's work," he said. Wanda examined the roll of money and smiled warmly at Jonathon.

Another bottle of champagne was called for and poured. Lady Louise, like one in a trance, held out her glass. She wanted to leave, but some strange fascination held her there. It was like a peek into some forbidden world. Hell, perhaps, or purgatory. And Salverton was quite at home with this motley crew. How had she been so mistaken about him?

"I'll hobble on down to Bow Street and see if they want a statement before I run along home," Jonathon said sometime later. "Be sure you look me up when you're in Brighton, melord. Always ready to serve—for a price. And you, Sammy. You know who to come to if your young man cuts up on you." He tossed a roguish grin at Salverton.

When he rose to leave, he cast a long look in Wanda's direction in a tacit invitation to join him. She didn't hesitate a minute before rising.

"I must be toddling along," she said, making a showy curtsy around the room. "I don't believe I caught your name, miss," she said to Lady Louise, who just stared. Miss! She had never been called miss in her life. "Is she simple?" Wanda asked Salverton in a perfectly audible aside.

Salverton ignored the question. He took Wanda's elbow, accompanied her and Jonathon out the door, and steered them into his study before leaving. He unlocked a metal box and drew out a considerable quantity of bills. "A little something for your trouble, Jonathon," he said.

"Generous to a fault, as always." Jonathon smiled.

Salverton handed Wanda a few bills. "My butler will find you a hackney, Miss Claridge. Most kind of you to have come."

"Any time, milord," Wanda said with an inviting leer.

"How did you get here, Jonathon?" Edward asked.

"I hired a gig at Newman's for the trip to Brighton, after Townsend sprung me. I'll drive this charming lady home. Wanda?"

"Going to Brighton, did you say?" Wanda asked.

"To check up on my business interests there. My inn—"

"Oh, my, you own an inn! I'd like to see it sometime."

"No time like the present."

"You don't waste any time," she said with a flirtatious smile.

"Time's not for wasting," he said, and grabbed her arm.

Salverton shook his head as they left, already halfway into negotiations for Wanda's favors. Jonathon was right as usual. Time wasn't for wasting. He'd wasted too long already.

When Salverton returned to the saloon, Lady Louise had recovered sufficiently to demand an explanation of these irregular goings-on. "Who were those yahoos, Salverton?" she demanded.

"Jonathon Sykes is a friend; Miss Claridge was involved in the arrest that occurred this morning. You need not concern yourself about her, Louise. I doubt we'll see her again."

"I certainly shan't, nor that other creature, either. I fear Papa would not like my meeting such low people. There is just one thing I should like to know before I leave. Is this young lady"—she glanced at Samantha—"married, or is she not?"

"Not at the moment," Salverton replied. "Wanda Claridge had designs on Samantha's brother. To be rid of her, we let on Samantha was Darren's wife. She is, in fact, his sister."

"I see. And why did you feel it necessary to pretend to me? I was not likely to meet Miss Claridge."

"One never knows. You just did meet her."

She gave him a long, searching look. "You've become very adept in juggling the truth, Salverton." She rose and took her leave of the remaining company. Salverton accompanied her to the hallway.

"You'll make a better politician than I ever thought," she said before leaving. "I take it you won't be attending my ball this evening?"

"I fear not. I can hardly leave my cousins alone."

"Of course," she said with great feeling.

"I'm sorry, Louise."

When he opened his lips to explain, she wafted her gloved hand in dismissal and nodded to Luten. "Good-bye, Salverton," she said in the accents of one who has narrowly escaped the gallows. Luten held the door open and she sailed out.

"Are you anticipating further callers, your lordship?" Luten inquired as he closed the door. "What I wish to ascertain is whom I should admit, and whom not?"

"I'm holding open house this morning, Luten. All comers are welcome."

Luten bowed, to conceal the movement of his lips. Lord Salty was back! This infernal tomb was livelier than it had been in a decade.

Samantha cast a sheepish look on Salverton when he returned. "I'm sorry about Wanda's coming, Edward," she said. "I had no idea Lady Louise would be here."

"When folks come uninvited, they can't complain of the company. I could hardly turn Jonathon from the door after all he's done for us."

Darren demanded an explanation of this intriguing statement. They were still discussing it when luncheon was announced, and they hadn't gotten around yet to mentioning that Wanda had a grown daughter. The explanations lasted through the whole meal.

When they were finished, Darren said, "Could I have a word with you in your study, Cousin? I find myself a trifle short—for the trip home, you know. Naturally, I'll repay every penny."

"Naturally, with interest," Salverton said, for he wanted Darren to realize the importance of responsibility. Salverton accompanied him out.

Miss Donaldson said to Samantha, "We should be getting home, Sam."

"To Oakbay, do you mean?"

"We'll stay the night at Upper Grosvenor Square and get an early start in the morning. Did Edward say anything . . ."

"About what?" Sam asked, but the flush that crept up her neck showed she realized very well what her chaperon meant.

"Did he offer for you?"

"Of course not! He's practically engaged to Lady Louise."

"I wonder . . ."

She was not left long in doubt when Salverton returned to say he would have his carriage deliver Miss Donaldson and Darren to Upper Grosvenor Square. He wished to take Samantha for a drive in the park to discuss matters. "With your permission, ma'am?" he added. "You are *in loco parentis.*"

"With my heartfelt approval!" she exclaimed, and kissed him on both cheeks, after which she turned as pink as a peony and emitted a girlish giggle.

Edward and Samantha went to the front door to see Darren and Miss Donaldson off. After they left, Samantha turned to Edward, suddenly shy. "Have you called for the carriage for our drive?" she asked.

"In a moment. There's something I want to say first." He drew her into the saloon. Over his shoulder he said to Luten, "I am no longer 'at home,' Luten." Then he closed the door.

Luten could not recall having seen that particular door closed since Lord Salty's disappearance. Behind the closed door, Salverton led Samantha to one of a pair of sofas flanking the fireplace, but they didn't sit down.

Samantha was overtaken by a fit of nerves. "I'm sorry, Edward," she said.

Salverton blinked in astonishment. Was it to be a refusal? "I haven't even asked you yet!" he exclaimed.

"Oh! I meant about Darren, and Wanda, and everything. I know such goings-on are not what you are accustomed to, or approve of. I cannot imagine what Lady Louise thinks."

"I cannot imagine caring what Lady Louise thinks."

"Of course you care! You're going to offer for her." She gazed at Edward with bated breath, trying to read his mind.

"I was going to offer for her—until you brought me to my senses." He seized her two hands and squeezed them.

"Oh, I am glad," she said, and drew a deep breath. "I could not but feel she was the worst possible match for you—although she is very pretty," she allowed.

"Even in the comatose state I've lived in these past years, I still insisted on some modicum of beauty in my ladies. But let us not speak of Louise."

"You wanted to ask me something . . ." she said, peering up at him with a question and such hope and love beaming in her eyes that Salverton forgot the question and crushed her into his arms for a kiss that left them both breathless.

As his lips bruised hers, the question was asked and answered to their mutual satisfaction. Samantha's head whirled with the unexpected passion and joy of that kiss. Edward loved her. He wanted to marry her, and if he hadn't asked, she would have died. She had resisted even calling on him until necessity forced her into it, and now she would marry him and be with him forever.

After a long kiss she opened her eyes, and saw him studying her intently. "I never even imagined such a thing," she sighed.

"I thought you were coming to realize I cared for you."

"I mean when I first came—or didn't come, to see you."

Edward appeared to understand this disjointed speech. "Stiff-rumped," he said. "I've changed."

"I noticed," she said with a trembling smile.

They were interrupted by a knock at the door. "I told him I wasn't at home!" Edward scolded.

Luten's apologetic voice came through the door. "I'm sorry to disturb you, your lordship, but it's Lord Liverpool."

Samantha gasped in excitement.

After a brief pause, Edward said, "Never mind that. It's only the prime minister," and kissed his fiancée again.